THE BEWILDERED

a novel by Peter Rock

THE BEWILDERED

a novel by Peter Rock

MacAdam/Cage

MacAdam/Cage Publishing
155 Sansome Street, Suite 550
San Francisco, CA 94104
www.macadamcage.com

Library of Congress Cataloging-in-Publication Data:

Rock, Peter, 1967—
     The bewildered : a novel / by Peter Rock.
          p.cm.
     ISBN 1-59692-112-9 (alk. paper)
     1. Children—Fiction. 2. Friendship—Fiction. 3. Portland
(Or.)—Fiction. 4. Underground areas—Fiction. I. Title

     PS3568.O327B49 2005
     813'.54—dc22

                                                    2004030828

Manufactured in the United States of America.

10 9 8 7 6 5 4 3 2 1

Book and jacket design by Dorothy Carico Smith.

ACKNOWLEDGMENTS
Deep gratitude to Ella Vining, the champion; love to all Vinings
(especially Motoko, for expertise in Japanese) and Rocks.
Thanks to Kate Nitze, David Poindexter and everyone at
MacAdam/Cage. A debt to Ira Silverberg. Susan Choi, Stacey
D'Erasmo and Whitney Otto are generous friends and sharp
readers. Thanks once more to Kate Nitze, sharpness itself.

for Ella

They created in a single night
a new situation and now it appeared
to bewilder them.
For the moment, their bewilderment was
their only etiquette.

—Yukio Mishima
The Sailor Who Fell from Grace with the Sea

ONE

1.

NATALIE LIKED TO WALK IN THIS RAIN. It tasted metallic to her, just a mist drifting down before six in the morning. The train tracks were slippery underfoot, the greasy wooden rails, and I-5 only fifty feet to her left, trucks rattling north to Seattle and beyond. Across the dark river, across the Burnside Bridge, a neon sign was visible—a leaping stag, the words *Made in Oregon*.

She walked with purpose, and fast, like a man with things to do. People often asked her if she was going somewhere; she had no patience for that question. She was straight adrenaline. She was electric, up all night.

The bridge spanned back toward her, toward the Towne Storage building with its dirty red brick and rows of dark windows, its black water tank pressed into the sky, its paintings of lions' heads, looking down. Lions were famously brave, and they lived together, in prides. She herself was alone, and proud, and brave.

Above, ahead, the Burnside Bridge crossed I-5, and 84 forked east, all the overpasses looping and swooping around each other, the colored cars blurring as they slipped past, the tiny round heads of people within, looking out.

These people could see Natalie, standing here, dressed like a man in her Dickies and work boots. She didn't know why she still wore her long, dark blond hair; she'd braided it twice, twisted it up under a baseball cap. She wore knee socks, like always, but the people above couldn't tell that. To them, she probably looked more like a boy than a man, her body wound tight as she walked, her ears pierced but without earrings; she couldn't always stand metal on her body—the back of her watch had burned a patch on her wrist, so she threw it away. Now she never knew what time it was; she guessed by the sun, when it was visible, which wasn't often. She could carry a watch in her pocket, perhaps, if there were room. Her right front pocket held a plastic barrette shaped like Daisy Duck, the keys to her truck, trailer and the storage locker, a chili recipe she'd never use, a Leatherman multipurpose tool, a shrill whistle in case of trouble. A pencil stub. A battery. Her other pockets held photographs of her girls.

The people in the cars might believe she was a girl or man or boy or woman, but they had no idea, they could have no clue what Natalie was up to, out this morning in the rain.

Scrub bushes and chain-link fences were the best places, the natural habitat. She looked past scraps of clothing, torn plastic and then, here, *Holy Crow!*, homed in on torn paper—the dull shine of a photograph, the color of skin, a promise. She kicked gravel, going after the scrap as if someone else might snatch it first. The paper was nicely worn, stiffened and damp in her fingers. It was not one of hers, and there was some excitement in that, a pleasure, a sentimental glimmer. The woman's face was torn in two; still she smiled. It was a piece of a Fred Meyer catalog, from the department store, depicting modest and high-waisted lingerie, a support bra that must weigh five pounds. The half-faced woman was someone's wife, some proud middle manager in Beaverton saying he was married to a model. Her body looked soft and inviting, her dark hair perfectly curled and clean. The disembodied hand of another woman reached toward this woman's bare shoulder; the two women had been having one of those underwear parties catalog people enjoyed, and then this friend had been torn away, perhaps more desired.

Natalie dropped the scrap, replaced it, left it behind for someone else to discover. Standing, she walked away, satisfied. There were only her footsteps and the sandpaper sound of her stiff denim jacket, her arms swinging as she turned right, away from the tracks and the interstate and the river. The smell of garbage seeped from dumpsters, laced with the exhaust in the air, sifting through the misty rain. Three blocks away on MLK, traffic lights turned green, tiny winking eyes.

She had three of her girls with her, all from 1976, all

folded in the pockets of her jacket. Yes, these ladies were over forty years old now, but she preferred them as they were, in 1976, wishing America Happy Birthday. She could still find the old magazines, in antique stores—some of the shop owners even held them out for her, the Bicentennial issues, in clear plastic covers, pages smelling of mold. They were often well preserved, but she roughed them up slightly before bringing them out. Sometimes she ripped her girls a little, and imagined the excited dissatisfaction of finding only the legs, the ass, the high heels. A faded face here, a breast there, a bare foot with a chain anklet, an ear, an expression of pain or pleasure, torn in two. That's how she had found them, and she knew some believed pornography was boring because it was artificial, yet the feelings she remembered were natural, too sharp and unexpected to be false.

Natalie did not slow her pace. Closer to the Burnside Bridge, closer to the shadows beneath it, past loading docks with their metal doors pulled down, red and blue squares against the lighter concrete. Abandoned streetcar tracks lined the asphalt; she stepped over them. A wheelchair was parked halfway under one dock, and someone slept on an old mattress under there, the dirty soles of his bare feet showing. She passed quietly, so as not to disturb him.

The lions overhead looked a little more like bears, high on the Towne Storage building. Natalie walked with, she carried Miss November, Patti McGuire, who stands in a fantasy Midwestern diner with all her dress's buttons undone, leaning against the jukebox, her unbelievable supple flesh all there for you, her stare a challenge. Patti loves CB radios; she exudes heat. And rubbing against her, paper to paper, is peroxided Miss May, in high snakeskin boots, one zipper already slipping, her bare ass pressing against the cold metal coin dispenser of a pinball machine, her nipples another set of startled eyes. And Deborah Borkman, Miss July, wearing knee-high striped socks and nothing else as she sets up a tent. Her body is dark and taut and thin, her hair blown back; her hands hold a thick rope that mysteriously hangs from above, as if she might climb straight to Heaven, where she belongs. Bathrooms, game rooms and barns—these girls have bodies, they want to show them off, and there often seems to be a rope nearby. Looping, stretched taut, or in the background; incidental, yet a continual possibility; coiled, as if holding electricity.

Natalie eased a hand into the pocket, felt the pages, the photographs, the girls. All this was like setting a trapline, with bait that could be blown away, burned up, lost. Only she was not trying to catch anything, anyone—was she? She was only trying to stay connected to a thrill, to cast one forward, to provide for someone what she'd once had.

A few deliveries were already being made. It was fruit mostly, down here. She approached a row of parked semi-trailers, *Pacific Coast Fruit Company* painted on their sides. Here, she slowed; she bent down. She reached into her jacket pocket and unfolded part of a centerfold, glimpsed only the red and black wool blanket, the canvas tent, and recognized it. The air smelled sweet, of rotten, fermenting fruit. She folded the already stiff paper, wedged it under the thick, black rubber of a tire, where the flash of skin would catch in the corner of someone's eye, reel them in.

Natalie stepped into the shadow, out of the rain, the blackened underside of the Burnside Bridge above her. Beneath the echoing roar of the traffic, she heard a strange sound. A solid, whirring hiss. It came, and it went. She paused, and cocked her ear. It was on her right, where a low wall stretched, its concrete spray-painted with hundreds of white skulls, solid, as if piled atop one another. And then the sound returned, swooped closer.

Suddenly, a head, a young girl's head slid along the top of the wall, her pale face intent, her long hair pulled back; the girl stared straight ahead, fiercely anticipating and yet calm, her head sliding from right to left, then gone, the sound fading.

Startled, Natalie stepped closer to the wall. She stretched and looked over: the girl was on a skateboard, rolling across smooth curves of concrete, carving up the walls, hands out, knees and elbows flexing, her wake almost visible in the morning shadows. The girl shot back up the steep slope of the near wall; the rails of the board slid along the top edge and she was gone again, her face hovering there for a split second between forward and backward, transfixed and looking into the next move, her bright eyes not even seeing Natalie.

Above, on the bridge's dark stanchions, a sign said no

alcohol was allowed at the skatepark. No camping, no vandalism, no abusive behavior. OVER ALL, BE A GOOD NEIGHBOR. While the sign said no graffiti, there were the skulls and, across where the tall wall rose—a hundred feet distant, where the bridge angled down—there were red and yellow flames, the silhouettes of the damned. A hooded Grim Reaper loomed in the foreground, his scythe twenty feet long.

The girl skated toward Natalie, then dropped into a tight, sunken, perfectly round bowl—its mouth twenty feet across—and circled quickly inside it, her feet as high as her head, her body parallel to the bottom; her face stared up, expressionless, her ponytail straight out, rigid, like the hand of a clock inside that round white space.

Natalie leaned in, wanting to be closer. Up near the Reaper, near the broken concrete atop the wall, she saw a space under the bridge, a path leading to it. A space where a person might stand and look down, and have a better view. The low walls at the corners had chain-link fence along the top, bent back here and there. She walked around, past dark scrawls where graffiti had been painted over, past more skulls, past the word FEAR in tall white letters. She scrabbled up the loose dirt and gravel, the broken-down concrete, and stood with her head near the bridge's blackened underside.

The exhaust fumes were stronger, mixed with the ashes of campfires long gone out, and the traffic's rattle and roar muted the sound of the girl's wheels below. The gray of the concrete was smooth, as if burnished, the color of an elephant's hide. The girl now balanced on one leg, pushed hard with the other for more speed, her shoe slapping. She wore headphones over her ears, and torn jeans, black sneakers, a long-sleeved white T-shirt, her body angular and small and never still, perfectly balanced, knees bending to pump the board higher up the wall and then gliding there, almost weightless. Natalie wanted to call out, to applaud, but she didn't want to interrupt, to break the concentration, the reverie. She forced her hands into her pockets and listened to the wheels, the rasp of the board's wooden tail against concrete.

The girl rose up the near wall, planted a hand down low and, wheels screeching, the board took her feet and legs up above her in a smooth arc, returning beneath her, beautiful.

Natalie heard a footstep behind her, then, a dragged scuffing sound, a low voice closer than it should be.

"Dope?" a young man asked. "Coke? Tweak?" His face was hooded, hands in the pockets of his huge jeans.

She shook her head, turned away, waved him off.

"I saw you earlier," he said. "I followed you, a little. No offense. You're looking for something—I can tell."

"I'm very busy," she said, her whispered voice strange to her. She turned to face him, and didn't want to look away from the girl. "Do you know her?"

"I'm just asking," he said. "Alls I'm saying is—"

"I have a knife," she said. "Do you want me to scream?"

"Jesus. What is your problem?" He backed off, just blinking his eyes at her. Then he turned the corner and climbed out of view.

The cars above had grown louder, heading into rush hour, and now there was no sound of the skateboard's wheels, no sign of the girl. Below, the concrete stretched gray, empty. Natalie looked to the right, across an abandoned parking lot. Three crows hopped along—black wings half out, tormenting each other, feathers shiny as if wet, lacquered. She hurried back down the slope, breathing hard, feet sliding in the scree, back around the walls of the skatepark.

The girl stood near the semi-trailers, faced away, not moving. Reading something she held in her hands, turning over the ragged page. The headphones were still on; Natalie crept closer, the sound of her footsteps covered. She tried to regain her breath, to slow down. She got within five feet, almost close enough to reach out and touch the girl's shoulder.

The girl spun and simultaneously shoved the paper into her pocket, pulled the headphones from her ears, around her neck, and twisted her face into a warning scowl.

"Hey," Natalie said. "Easy."

She noticed that she was a head taller than the girl, and that the girl's part was purposefully crooked, like a sharp lightning bolt in her dirty blond hair. Her thick eyebrows were almost grown together. Her face was so white, her lips pale and chapped. Her blue eyes didn't blink. She bent down and picked up her skateboard with one hand; in the other, she held a black case, long and narrow.

"What's in there?" Natalie said.

"My flute." The girl's voice was surprisingly husky.

"What were you reading, there?"

"Nothing."

"You sure can skate. I watched."

The girl shrugged. There were illegible ballpoint scribbles, blue, on the rubber toes of her shoes. The bottom of her skateboard faced Natalie—the wheels were deep orange, the metal of the trucks ground down. Deep scratches marked the flames of the paint job; the word BEWILDERED had been written there with a marker.

"What's that mean?" Natalie said, pointing.

"I don't know. My friend did it."

"Are you safe, down here alone, so early?"

"Whatever," the girl said.

Natalie smiled as the silence settled between them. She knew it was partially that the girl was intrigued by her, but mostly that she didn't want to show fear. She wouldn't run, not right away. The smell of overripe fruit hung thick in the air.

"What were you listening to?" Natalie said.

"Japanese."

"What?"

"Language tapes," the girl said. "To learn to speak it." The cuffs of her white shirt had holes cut in them, her thumbs hooked there, pulling the sleeves taut. Her body was a boy's body, almost; it was just beginning to stray, to betray itself, to become what it would be. It was caught in a delicious balance.

"I thought I saw you reading something," Natalie said. "Before."

Again, the girl shrugged.

"I thought I saw you looking at Deborah Borkman."

"Who?"

"She won her first beauty contest, a neighborhood affair, when she was nine. She likes to climb trees, and gardening."

The girl listened, confused, recognizing the lines from the magazine page.

"If it's yours," she said, reaching for her pocket, "you can have it."

"No," Natalie said. "No, no. It's not like that. You can keep her."

"What?"

"Debbie Borkman." Natalie reached into her jacket pocket and pulled out another photograph, from the same pictorial; Miss July stood outdoors in a washtub, taking great pleasure from her bath, inviting onlookers to do the same. With her stub of pencil, Natalie wrote her own phone number—copying it from another slip of paper—across Deborah's lovely stomach. She handed the page across to the girl.

"So what?" the girl said, putting it in her pocket.

"There's some things I need help with," Natalie said.

She half-surprised herself with this gesture, these words; they were not premeditated. "Could you help me?" she said. "There would be pay, of course."

The girl dropped her skateboard down on its wheels, one foot atop the black grip tape. She unhooked her thumb, stretched her arm, checked the watch on her wrist.

"Could my friends do it, too?" she said.

"Call me," Natalie said. "We'll figure it out."

"School." The girl pointed down the street, kicked her board around. "Dozo yoroshiku," she said, and began to roll away.

"All right, then," Natalie called after her. "I'll see you soon."

Alone again, she headed back out from under the bridge. Was the rain picking up? She told herself not to care; natives didn't even notice, they seemed born with gills. She walked, alert, her eyes searching, nose twitching, head jerking from side to side. If they were out here, she would find them.

Another lingerie catalog would be enough—she wasn't greedy. She did not like the hardcore, however; she preferred some softness, some pride and suggestion. Her favorites were the old *Playboys*, like the ones she'd first found, twenty-five years ago. She could tell that her memory was not strong, but memories sometimes came all at once, and the important ones repeated, vividly—she had been a girl in Denver when she came upon the magazines; in a city park, under a bush; someone's stash, some boy her age or slightly older, stolen from some father or uncle (*Entertainment for Men*—that subtitle deliciously raising the stakes). This was back during the Bicentennial; Natalie was twelve and tender and caught up with the ideas of freedom and possibility, her body testifying, not really developed but hinting toward the promise that the women, the Playmates demonstrated in their poses, their freedom, there in the seventies when it wasn't ironic. They believed and she believed, a girl holding the rain-stiff, ripped magazines, hoarding the photographs and memorizing the women's names. She had never felt better, more excited and full of anticipation than then, and as she walked through the rain this morning she sensed some of that same energy.

2.

CHRIS HAD SCRAPED HIS ELBOW. He bent it up so Kayla and Leon could look at it; Leon frowned, and Kayla—the tip of her tongue between her teeth, the jagged part in her hair shining—looked disappointed. The wound was not as serious as they had hoped. It really wasn't swelling or bleeding the way they would have liked. It hadn't even been an impressive wipe-out, either—he was simply dropping in off the low wall, and his board went out from under him.

The skatepark beneath the bridge had been crowded, like it always was in the late afternoon, full of older guys with tattoos and stocking caps and pierced eyebrows. Of the three friends, Kayla was the best skater, by far, but she had trouble getting in rides without someone cutting her off. She'd been the only girl at the park; that was why she practiced so early in the morning, hours before school.

"Where is she?" Leon said to Kayla.

"She's coming."

"She's never been late before."

"And it's a school night," Chris said.

The air felt heavy, muggy. This would be the fifth night they'd worked for Natalie in the last month, and still they were anxious. The three of them stood at the curb on East Burnside and MLK, waiting, each with a backpack of books, each with an instrument case in one hand, a skateboard in the other. Leon was taller, bigger than the other two, but this had not always been the case. They'd met in fourth grade, set apart as gifted students in a program called Horizons; that was more than five years ago, and now all three were fifteen, in high school, inseparable. Over time they'd developed a sharp disdain for their peers, especially as these peers began the slide toward the superficial, pathetic lives of adults. The three believed that there had to be a less desperate way to live one's life, and this last twist—this Natalie, found by Kayla—felt especially promising.

Kayla sat down on her board, rolling slightly from side to side, her feet on the ground, knees bent up. Leon skated away with his trombone case over his shoulder, up half a block, searching, demonstrating that he wasn't afraid of the Mexican men who stood there in a group, smoking and speaking Spanish, here in this gathering place like so many others. This was where someone came when they needed illegal, cheap labor, some night work somewhere, off the books. The men didn't even notice as Leon rolled past, as he skidded the tail of his board, stopped, did a one-eighty, and skated back to Chris and Kayla. He pointed back to the intersection, at the stop light, the rusted-out pickup idling half a block away.

"There," he said, and already Kayla was standing.

As usual, Natalie drove her broken-down Ford slowly past, as if they had no pre-arranged meeting, as if she were looking for the best possible laborers. A man up the street yelled something in Spanish, stepped off the curb and flexed his arm. Natalie drove past, then stopped, then reversed slowly to where the three stood. She left the engine idling, like every time, as she got out to look them over.

Her long, blond hair hung straight and loose. Her boots were black, heavy. She wore blue coveralls, long sleeved, a zipper up the front.

"You appear to be very hard workers," she said. "Certainly." She looked up and down the street and the Mexican men glanced back, interested.

"Yes," Kayla said.

"Of course," Natalie said, "you seem very young to me."

This was all part of it; it was impossible to say if Natalie was kidding at all, or if she forgot, as if it were slightly more than coincidence yet new to her every time. She stood still for a moment, thinking, her old truck—two-tone, brown and white—rattling next to her.

"My name is Natalie," she said, "and you have never seen me before."

"Never," Leon said, and Kayla elbowed him in the side.

"The job I have for you," Natalie said, "this job is not

especially difficult; I will not ask you to break the law or do anything that you don't want to do. All I ask is secrecy."

As she spoke, she walked around the back of the truck. A fiberglass top covered the bed. She opened its hatchback, then the truck's tailgate.

"Your name?"

"Kayla."

"Kayla, I'd like you to ride up front with me. You boys in the back."

Leon and Chris tossed in their packs, their instrument cases, and their skateboards, then crawled in after. The truck's bed was covered by a piece of plywood, a scrap of old, orange shag carpet that smelled of dust and yarn, old sun. The two boys stretched out flat as Natalie closed them in. After a moment, the truck began moving.

"'I will not ask you to break the law,'" Leon said, and snorted. "Right." Flat on his back, he clasped his hands behind his head. He closed his eyes.

Leon's hair was black, curly, and there were dark freckles across his nose. He hated to be called "husky," but that's what he was, and strong, his arms and legs muscled, his wrists thick, his movements always slow and calm. He could sleep anywhere. Chris rested on his side, looking at his friend, then rolled onto his back. He stretched out, lining up his feet with Leon's, then dragged himself up, so they were the same height, lying there with their shoulders touching. He kept his eyes open, staring up at the cracks in the white fiberglass shell.

The truck jerked and jolted, the shock absorbers shot. Chris sat up, to check where they were. They'd crossed the river now and were still on Burnside, traveling through downtown, climbing up a slope. He looked forward, at the back of Natalie's head; her hair was swept to one side, and he could see her necklace, just four or five thin copper wires against the pale skin of her neck. Two panes of glass separated the front of the truck from the back, two sliding windows there; last time Natalie had opened them, handed pieces of beef jerky back to Chris and Leon. Today she looked straight ahead. Kayla, meanwhile, sat with a heavy book in her lap, reading, probably about electricity. That was her deal—the hard science, the numbers; Chris was better at history, at English; Leon specialized in music, in debate, but he could do it all. Now, he slept.

Chris squinted through the two windows. He saw writing on Kayla's hand, ballpoint pen. *LEON*, it said; why hadn't he noticed that before? And why not his name, too? He checked her other hand. It was bare, unmarked. Then he watched as Kayla leaned forward and changed the radio's channel; her shirt rode up, and he saw the almost nonexistent hairs at the small of her back, in a crescent there like a rising sun. The soft hairs of his own arm rose in a shiver. He knew that Kayla wished the hair on her own arms was blonder, so it wouldn't show; he knew that she'd just started shaving her legs. He pressed his ear against the window and heard something, past the truck's rattle; it sounded like a classical station, some cheesy Mozart. His head facing out, he looked through the porthole window of the fiberglass shell. A cemetery, a hillside of white grave-stones, flashed against the dark sky. It was going to rain; Natalie never had work for them when the weather was decent.

Chris checked his elbow again; there was a disap-pointing lack of blood, and what there had been had already dried. It wouldn't even be a decent scab.

"Well?" Leon said, his eyes still closed.

"Heading toward Beaverton, maybe."

"You want to quiz me on my Biology?"

"Not right now," Chris said.

"What are you doing?"

"Thinking."

"Did you finish *The Sound and the Fury*?"

"Over-rated," Chris said.

Leon sat up, rubbing at his eyes, looking from side to side. "It's a good thing she has a lid on this thing," he said. "You know, dogs that ride in the back of trucks are always getting their retinas detached; they go blind. There's a whole area in any Humane Society, any dog pound. Cages and cages of these blind dogs. Rednecks' dogs, mostly."

As he spoke, he pulled his instrument case toward him and undid the hasps. He opened it; instead of his trom-bone, it held all the equipment that Natalie had given them to keep. All the straps and ropes and buckles and gloves. The orange phone headset spilled out, trailing its cords, alligator clips at the ends. Kayla said she was going to figure out how it worked; she was reading up on it, on the Internet.

"I saw Kayla change the radio channel," Chris said.

"Perfect. What did Natalie do?"

"Nothing. How old do you think she is?"

"Too old to trust," Leon said.

Out the window, strip malls and new condo developments trailed off. Open fields stretched; cows and sheep, green grass.

"So what do we think her deal is?" Chris said.

"We're still gathering information."

"I know that."

"It's interesting," Leon said. "We've all agreed on that. Not boring, yet."

"Yet," Chris said.

Natalie skidded to a stop on the highway's gravel shoulder; Chris and Leon jostled against each other, just sitting upright again as she jerked the back doors open.

"Out!" she said. "Line up, now."

This was part of it. The skateboards were left behind in the truck, the backpacks, with Chris's clarinet and Kayla's flute. Chris stood between Leon and Kayla, facing Natalie, who was excitedly pacing, pointing up and down the highway, at the setting sun, the darkening fields, the black wires between metal towers.

"Beautiful," Natalie said. "What time is it, now?"

"Eight," Chris said.

"I'll be back at ten," she said.

"Nine-thirty," Kayla said. "It's a school night."

"All right," Natalie said, turning away, looking over her shoulder. "Don't disappoint me!"

And then she leapt back into the truck, slammed her door and accelerated away, gone.

"Whoa," Leon said. "Was she acting that crazed the whole drive?"

"Not really," Kayla said. "She was just talking."

"She wasn't even wearing a watch," Chris said.

"What was she talking about?" Leon said.

The three friends sat on the shoulder of the highway, alone for miles in every direction, fields stretching out. They began to untangle the harness, the ropes. There was not the slightest hint of a breeze. The power lines ran between metal towers, their tops spread in triangles and with smaller metal triangles like ears on top, so they looked like the faces of cats. The wires stretched over low, distant hills, trees clear-cut to make way.

"Oh, man," Kayla said. She pointed across the street, to where the lines ran between regular wooden poles. "Not on this side. Let's go over there, where at least the voltage has been stepped down some. What's she thinking? Holy crow!"

"What kind of expression is that?" Leon said. "'Holy crow?'"

"Are you going to disallow it?"

"Not yet."

The three had rules about clichés and hip phrases, and did not allow cursing.

"So what was Natalie talking about?" Chris said.

"Nothing," Kayla said. "Creepy questions about being a girl, about which one of you was my boyfriend, just ridiculous and stupid adult stuff."

"She's just another adult," Leon said, "but she pays us, so she's working for us as much as we're working for her."

The horizon flickered; faint thunder sounded; above, the stars were becoming visible.

"Is this smart?"

"Not really."

The three hurried across the highway, into the tall grass. They continued their preparations, watchful for headlights, their voices low. They only understood some of the equipment; Natalie had given it to them in a bag that said Qwest on it, so it was clear that she'd stolen it from the phone company. They admired that.

"I could do the next one," Chris said, "or the one after that."

"We'll see if I get tired," Leon said. His feet were the biggest, so the spikes fit him best. He liked to be the one to climb the poles; once he got up there, he'd start to boss them around.

The spikes were hard to walk in, like having long knives attached to your ankles, stabbing into the ground with each step. Chris and Kayla helped Leon to his feet, then to the pole; they got the thick canvas belt around it, then through the harness, and boosted him up. Spikes dug into the wood, Leon slid the belt up, leaned back, dug a little higher. Slowly, he ascended, pausing to pull splinters from his palms. He had forgotten the gloves. Below, Chris and Kayla set to hiding the trombone case, the things they wouldn't need, and then they returned, ready.

"Only the neutrals!" Kayla shouted, hands belled around her mouth, "don't touch the live wires with the cutter."

"Right, right, right." Leon's whispered voice hardly reached them. "The air is hotter up here."

"What?"

"Forget it." He put his small, metal flashlight in his mouth, so he could get to work.

The first time, Natalie had explained it so fast that it was surprising they hadn't killed themselves. Each time they knew a little more, and Kayla read about it, so they were a little better at what they had to do.

Leon cut the neutral, the grounding wire that ran with the live ones; it went with a snap and the pole swayed, settled, that tension gone; the heavy copper wire came down like a whip, cracking up and out, winding and unwinding around the other wires and back upon itself, stiff and slackening, coming down.

Kayla and Chris ran after it, racing each other to get the very end. Then, as Leon descended behind them, they began to bend the wire, to roll it into a ball, larger and larger. Chris balled it up, and Kayla lifted the wire from the tall grass, to keep it clear.

When these skeins of wire grew more than a foot in

diameter, they became heavy, more difficult to carry. By that time, Leon would have climbed down behind them, taken off the spikes, and caught up with the clipper. He cut the wire, and they set the heavy skein aside and began to roll another, all the way to the next pole, which Leon would climb so they could finish this stretch and begin the next. Now, they kept an eye out for headlights; this highway was not heavily traveled. The night was still, the air close. A cow, grazing nearby, moaned low. It lifted its black and white head and blankly stared at Chris and Kayla.

"Dude's watching us."

"Concentrate on what you're doing," Kayla said.

"She could help us," he said. "Natalie. She could at least stick around."

"Too risky. Besides, she's an adult. What do you expect?"

"I wonder where she goes."

–⋀⋁⋀–

Natalie sat in a booth, in a roadside diner, watching the trucks pass on the highway, wondering how her kids were doing out there. Before she had entered the diner, she had gotten out of her coveralls. She wore a silk, flowered blouse and sandals with blue straps, an outfit that owed something to Whitney Kaine, Miss September, 1976.

"Are you ready to order?"

Natalie looked up at the waitress, who wore a hemp necklace, a tattooed ring on her finger.

"Strange weather," the girl said, eager to fill any silence. "Are you visiting the vineyards? Passing through?"

"Business," Natalie said.

"What do you do?"

"Maybe I'll have a steak. Do you have any vegetables that came in tin cans?"

"Only fresh vegetables; we're an organic restaurant."

Natalie could not remember the last time she ate a fresh piece of fruit, or a vegetable; she liked the hint of metal in the canned versions, but even they were not a major part of her diet.

"And we don't serve any meat," the waitress said.

"Just give me anything. The first thing on the menu."

"Pardon me?"

"I'm not hungry."

"You don't really have to order anything."

"Yes, but I'd like to sit here, I'd like to pay you for the time and space. Does that strike you as suspicious?"

"Do you like things that are hot, spicy?" the waitress said, trying.

"I used to," Natalie said.

"I'll bring you the special," the waitress said. "It's eggplant, but I bet you'll like it."

Natalie turned away, back to the window. She had no time, no patience for chatter, weather talk, petty divulgements of opinions or vocation. What did she do? How did she come to her current employment? Is that what it was, when she gave away all the earnings to the children, her workers? Number Six hard-drawn copper was running sixty cents a pound, two hundred and forty dollars a mile, at worst. All that mystery she worked on the kids, all that drama and commando bullshit wasn't really necessary, but she knew exactly how to play them, and didn't mind feeding their attitude, their sense of superiority. She liked their serious, dependable way, how they acted like miniature experts, how little respect they actually showed her.

She checked the clock on the wall. Forty-five minutes left. A school night, they said, they had to get home and get their sleep to be sharp for school, for classes. Sleep. She used to need more of it. She wasn't tired now; she felt the same, plenty of energy, even too much. She'd go days without sleeping, even thinking about it. And then she'd sleep for forty, fifty hours straight, and be up for a week. Scientists admitted they didn't know why people needed it. Dolphins slept half of their brain at a time, otherwise they'd drown; perhaps that was how she was doing it— never all the way asleep or awake.

Alone in the diner, she felt the pressure rising, a faint hot wind from the faces of the electrical outlets, invisible and silent sparks, all closing down, rushing in, a surge snaking toward her. Snarled, forked, bristling and gone slack. In came a snapping hiss at all the switches and light fixtures, and she heard the cook drop something in the kitchen. She heard his cursing voice as all the lights went out.

—⋁⋀⋎—

There was no rising, sizzling wind, no spark, no ball of flame. Just a sudden loud pop and Leon jerking there like all the bones gone from his body, so high above the ground. His arms wildly slapped and his legs kicked the pole, gouging the wood, raining splinters into their squinting eyes. It went on and on; it would not set him loose. The heavy clipper was clenched in his hand still, shattering porcelain insulators, knocking crossbeams loose. The cut copper wire came slicing down.

Kayla screamed. She collided into Chris; they both looked upward, necks bent back as at last Leon came loose. His spikes kicked in, he slid in the harness, twisting in the canvas belt, forty feet overhead. He slid five feet, snagged, slid a little more. His eyes wide open, not seeing a thing, facedown and slithering closer, right at them, headfirst and tangled, finally hung up four feet from the ground.

They both held back; neither wanted to touch him, his pale face with all the skin twitching, hissing flecks of spit and snot, eyes staring. His limp arms hung down, his hand finally letting loose of the clipper, its damp thud in the grass. At last, Kayla reached out, then Chris. They brought their friend down to the ground.

"Is he breathing?" Chris said. "Is he alive?"

Leon was not moving. Now even the skin of his face settled and smoothed, eyelids sliding closed.

Kayla knelt next to him. She tilted back his head, opened his mouth. She pinched her nose and breathed into him, and checked to see his chest rise, and did it again, gasping herself.

She waited, and Leon's chest rose without her.

"He's all right," Chris said. "He'll be all right."

"He tastes burnt," Kayla said.

Leon pulled up his arms; he put his folded hands under his cheek, as if he were sleeping. All his hair was singed away on one side. He began to twitch again, his limbs faintly jerking. His jaw opened; he ground his teeth as if he were chewing, then swallowed like he was drinking. His eyes rolled, then closed again.

A car rattled by, not slowing. They did not notice. A warm wave of rain passed over them, then eased.

"It had to be lightning," Kayla said, repeating it. "Miles away where we didn't see it. Lightning, lightning." She was trying to get the belt, the spikes off him, as if that would help.

"Don't touch me," Leon said, suddenly. He sat up, twisting his head from side to side, his expression confused.

"Can you hear me? I'm right here."

"What? Who?"

"Wait, Leon. Stay down."

Chris looked over at Kayla, who looked back at him, both of them lost in that moment. A cool wind swept through the tall grass, around them. And then Natalie was there. They had not heard her truck, nor seen it arrive.

"Let's go!" she was saying, "What's the slowdown, here? What's up with your hair? Was it that way before?"

Chris kept looking at Kayla, not certain what to say.

"Yes," Kayla said. "It was that way." Her flashlight was in her jeans' pocket, forgotten, still on; it shone, a darker blue circle through the fabric.

Leon turned his head and looked at them with dawning recognition.

"Is everything all right?" Natalie said. "We need to get the wire in the truck, and then get out of here. We're compromising the whole situation."

"We're resting," Chris said. "We've got three balls done."

"Resting?" Natalie said. "What about that last wire?" She pointed to it, loose in the tall grass, weighing it down, the wire that Leon had cut just as things went wrong.

"Yes," Leon said, his voice thick and slow. "Well, let's go now."

He seemed about to tilt, to fall over on his side, but then began to crawl toward the rolls of wire; after fifty feet he stumbled up, barely walking, and Chris and Kayla trailed, staying close to help him and to keep Natalie from seeing. But she was not paying attention; she was out ahead, already stripping the wire with long, powerful jerks, tearing it up from the grass and coiling it. She still wore her coveralls, only now instead of her black boots she was in blue sandals, and she swayed to keep her balance as she gathered the last of the wire.

"Headlights!" she suddenly shouted. "Truck!" And they all fell flat in the long, wet grass, waiting, holding their breaths.

The rain had stopped; a swirling wind kicked up. The four of them rose again, all converging on the truck, each carrying one heavy skein, long strands of green grass snagged in the copper wire. Somehow Leon had also gathered the belt, the clippers, the headset, the trombone case. The bottom of his left shoe was blackened, the sole flapping; Chris stepped in front, so Natalie wouldn't notice. But she was already lifting the wire, rolling the balls into the back of the truck.

"We'll all ride back here," Kayla said.

"Suit yourselves."

They crawled in, over the tailgate, pressed close together, damp and safe, crowded by the skateboards and backpacks and wire. Natalie's face was visible for a moment, through the back window as she closed it down, and then there was the sound of the engine, the feel of the highway passing beneath them. The balls of wire began to roll around the back of the truck, bristly, catching on their clothing, pulling at their hair; the three sat with their feet outstretched, holding the wire away. They leaned into each other; they held each other close.

3.

NATALIE SAT IN THE CAB OF HER TRUCK, parked later that same night, once again on East Burnside, watching her children skate away. Her black boots stood on the seat next to her, the sandals on her feet a nightmare to drive in— she'd been in a hurry after the blackout, eager to check on the children, to see how involved they were. And something was up with those three, something; they were too scared to admit it, happy with their secrecy and that was fine, none of it mattered except that they got the wire, wire she had hopes for. She chuckled as she watched them disappear—laden with their backpacks, their instrument cases, staying tight together as they rolled down the sidewalk, startling pedestrians.

She shifted into gear, eased into the sparse nighttime traffic, turned south on MLK, past the Mexican restaurants and strip clubs, the clown supply warehouse. The girl, Kayla, had switched the radio to this terrible classical station, and now Natalie spun the dial into static. Once, perhaps, she'd been able to listen to classical, even enjoy it on a wound-up night like this; she suddenly recalled that she had really used to love the blues; names came from nowhere—Buddy Guy and Robert Johnson and Johnny Winter. These days she couldn't really bear any music; she preferred the static, the bristles rising and twisting higher, magnetic as the storms passed over. As she drove she could hear the balls of wire, cutting through the static: they rolled their way around the bed of the truck—a scratching, a muffled ricochet—as if charged and trying to work their way free.

She was ravenous! She accelerated, swooping up the Tacoma exit, then back over MLK, toward her place off Johnson Creek. She passed through the dark streets, the run-down houses, the wet dogs with their raspy, worn-down voices. The street she lived on went from blacktop to gravel to dirt; she could drive the last eighth of a mile with her eyes closed, and often practiced doing so.

Her only neighbor was an abandoned, boarded-up house, and her trailer wasn't even a double-wide, and it wasn't level, cinderblocks sinking into the soft ground. Pale blue, with a white stripe under the windows, rusted, dented on the far side where it likely tipped over in some past transport. She liked the sense that her house, too, had a past, that it had lived other places, housed other people and possibilities.

She skidded under the tall cedar, switched off the ignition, the radio static out of her ears and—boots in hand, truck door slamming, chain-link gate dragged open—she kept moving. Clumps of crabgrass made up the yard, growing around the previous tenants' bottle caps, shreds of magazines left out to cure and weather. The broken screen door hung loose, ready for her to clatter past, to push the storm door and then step on top of the for-warded letters, the job offers, the flyers from credit card companies.

She hit all the switches. She liked the lights bright, flu-orescent, flickering so fast no one could tell they weren't steady. She was home, here where no one could hide; the weight of a footstep was felt, wherever you were. Two bed-rooms, a living-dining area separated from the kitchen by a bar, and the bar and table covered in magazines, the way she liked it.

She jerked open the refrigerator, mixed herself a glass of weak Tang, just orange-tinted water, and tore into a Slim Jim, chewing fiercely as she poured water into a pot, put it on to boil. As she was getting it all going, getting past the initial craving, the shakiness, she paged through a magazine—April 1976, Denise Michele in a grass hut, near a rope hammock, no surprise. Her legs are shorter than most, her skin darker (though the lines of her string bikini are evident; not everyone gets to see all this), her left hip cocked up and her striped sarong held open as if she's taking it off, dropping it on the floor or about to put it on, tie it, though now she won't, now that she's been startled—

her expression is surprised, pleasantly surprised, her wide eyes, her long black hair on her bare, smooth shoulders as she stands next to that bamboo ladder, her right arm glistening, still wet.

The pot was boiling over! Natalie turned, angry, impatient with herself. She dialed down the burner, tried to find the foil packet. What if someone were watching this, through the windows? What would they understand? She went to close the blinds at the windows—the windows frozen shut in their screeching tracks—and there were no blinds so instead she turned out the lights, and then switched them back on, and returned to the stove. Mostly, she felt as good as she ever had, better, but sometimes she did only the things she found herself already doing, and she only wished she could anticipate the days she'd be sharp and the days she wouldn't.

Boiling again. She boiled curries and potatoes in foil packets. She ate dried fruit roll-ups, energy bars. Astronaut food. She thought of it as her astronaut diet; she never sat down to eat; like now, she bounced around the kitchen, imagining she was in zero gravity. Her throat, the cilia there, had to work extra hard to keep all the food from jerking back out of her, floating around the room. As she floated, as she chewed and swallowed, she held open the magazine with her free hand and read, and looked closely at the bamboo ladder next to Denise Michele. It's lashed together, not nailed—that would be inauthentic, but it is authentic, as real as Denise's expression, her face so hopeful, she has freedom and can taste it, the future impossible to know and yet unavoidably delightful, a limitless promise; and she's proud of her breasts with good reason, round and high and full, the undersides pale (the same bikini), the dark nipples that she is eager to share. She is innocent, surprised without her clothes, but happy to be surprised this way, naturally, not at all ashamed.

The phone was ringing. Natalie did not recognize it, at first. It took a moment to find it, beneath another magazine.

"Natalie," the man said. "Did you have success, this evening? My sources at the facility saw no new wire there."

"Holy crow," she said. "I forgot—"

"I can't have you forgetting."

"No," she said. "Yes. I mean, what I meant was that I didn't forget, that I did have success, that I only forgot to drop off the wire. I got caught up. I had success. It's still in the truck."

"You know what to do, then," the man said. "And when I'd like you to do it."

Natalie hung up the phone. She looked at the beads of water on Denise's breasts, her throat, at her glistening right arm, trying to figure it; past the waterfall, the grand piano—two pages back, there, she is in the bath; a bubble bath that is another reason to be hopeful, for anticipa- tion—not that she isn't always clean; she washes for fun, for pleasure, the way she wrings the washcloth so the bub- bles catch here and there—

The phone rang again, just once, as if to remind Natalie,

startle her loose.

—and yes, there were things to do. Yes, yes. The food she'd been chewing was suddenly tasteless in her mouth. The wire. She had had success. Miss April! She set Denise Michele aside, they'd meet another time, no doubt, back in 1976, in Hawaii. Denise is Hawaiian after all, the forty-ninth state and the freedom more recent, fresher, more appreciated and demonstrated, as she herself demonstrates it; she's been working as a Polynesian dancer, had a bit part in an episode of *Hawaii Five-O*. She has a fiery temper, but she can also be affectionate and sensual, and yet Natalie had to put her aside, had to get out of these sandals, into those boots, and out the door, across the yard, toward the truck.

She opened the back, jerked the tailgate so it bounced open, flat. Crawling inside, she reached out to touch the four balls of wire her children had harvested for her. Three were ordinary, only average, but the fourth ball, the last wire, was of a different grade—completely different and wonderful, still humming deep within. She pressed her cheek against it, then felt for the sharpened, cut end, then unwound the thinnest strand, thin as a hair yet stronger, for twenty inches; she bent it back and forth until it loosened, weakened, gave way; then she twisted it into a loop, tied it around her neck for strength.

She had to drive! What was she doing? Outside again, closing the back, climbing into the cab, she found the key, fired the ignition, accelerated out onto the dirt road. The truck roared, jerking sleeping dogs awake, back out through the neighborhood, retracing her path up MLK. She twisted the rearview mirror. The balls of copper wire were still waiting, anxious. She had forgotten, almost. The man had reminded her. Forgetfulness wasn't a bad thing, necessarily, but it could make things difficult. What did she really need to remember? In the trailer she had a drawer of facts—her name, her bank accounts, a calendar where she marked down the times the man told her, the places. Sometimes she even forgot about the drawer, and then opened it by chance and surprised herself, and remembered. Forgetfulness disconnected the past from the future, took her in a different direction, and she suspected that this was not something she could always deny. For the temptation was *not* to remember, to really forget, to embrace her best days, like lately when she felt as free as her girls look free, moving forward, her energy multiplying, never lapsing.

Could she forget to forget? Fall into habit and routine? Was forgetting to forget actually remembering? She had to be brave! To move forward, not to circle back. Yet in her pocket she still carried her address, though she almost never forgot that, and her phone number. The man had called, to remind her. How did he find her? Did she find him? That was back in those early, difficult days, right after she'd moved to Portland. After a night when she went out, when she had lost some time, where she woke up the next morning with a phone number in her pocket. He had opportunities for her, he'd told her. He understood her situation. He didn't want any commitment, they would never meet, he would always call her and not the other way around. She'd tried his number again, weeks later, and it had been disconnected; still, he knew how to reach her and did. He paid her promptly, too, with a receipt, as if this were all legal.

4.

THE THREE RODE THE MAX, the blue line, the train sliding west out of the city and speeding through the dark buildings. It was just after midnight, and Kayla sat between Leon and Chris, her knees knocking each of theirs. The boys had to lie to be out this late, but not Kayla; she lived with her father, who worked the night shift and slept most of the day. Her freedom was rarely compromised.

On buses, the three always sat in the very back, shoulder to shoulder; on the MAX, they went as far to the rear as they could without having to face backward. They liked to be able to see where they were headed.

"So I heard this story," Kayla said. "No, forget it."

There was only one other passenger on the MAX, five seats ahead of them—a tall, skinny man with his long legs bent out into the aisle, his narrow, black leather shoes stretching to sharp points. His black beard was also pointed, hooking down his jaw, meeting in a sharp V beneath his mouth. He may have been sleeping; he may have been watching them through the slits of his eyes.

"Tell it," Leon said.

"No," Kayla said. "You're not going to like it."

"Whatever," Chris said, "but you can't come halfway like that, you know we have a policy—"

"All right," she said. "Anyway, I heard about this guy, somewhere down in California, whose dick was so long it would drag on the ground when he walked—"

"Who told you this?" Chris said.

"Don't interrupt," Leon said. "Remember, Kayla decided we had to hear this."

"So," Kayla said, "this guy, just to walk down the street, had to wrap his thing around and around his leg, tie it there. But then one day he saw something that made him get a hard-on, and you know what happened?"

The two boys just stared at her, faces serious, trying to appear bored.

"It broke his leg in three places," she said.

No one said anything; the subject matter of Kayla's story—or joke, or whatever it was—had raised a temporary uneasiness between them. They had a policy about this; they didn't talk about sex. Of course, they had codes about sex itself, any kind of attraction. It was banned, especially between the three of them.

Kayla's jeans had a hole in the knee, the edges frayed; on her smooth, pale skin was the chalky circle of a lost scab, and her name written in red ballpoint, and another word or two that were mostly hidden, that Chris could not make out. He turned away from her, stared at his own reflection in the window. His hair seemed dark, cut this short, and he looked younger, his head smaller. He ran his hand over the smooth bristles. He had gone with Leon to have his head shaved, for solidarity; the accident, just a week before, had left Leon with hair on only one side. He had to even it out. When Chris had asked the barber how much it cost to get a shave, the barber had condescended, as adults liked to do, saying *For you? I could put a little cream on there, under your nose, bring my cat in here to lick it off.*

"I didn't tell you that story because I thought it was interesting," Kayla said. "But because someone else thought so. That's what's interesting about it. Pathetic."

"Still," Chris said, "you see how everyone acts at school—you give yourself over to that, it forces all the thoughts out of your head."

"And as soon as you start copulating," Leon said, "you can have children, of course—and then you might become a *parent*."

"It's not completely their fault," Kayla said.

"They should have seen it coming."

"And we'll become just like them if we're not careful," Chris said.

"Maybe, maybe not," Leon said.

"Unless," she said, "unless we can figure out another way to be."

"Right, right, right."

Ahead, the skinny, bearded man straightened his long legs, all the way across the aisle. He stretched his neck, twisting his face toward them, then away again.

"It was just a stupid story," Kayla said. "Probably wasn't even true."

"Definitely wasn't," Chris said.

The three sat, silent again, waiting, their skateboards propped against their knees, grip tape scratching rough against their jeans. They all skated Santa Cruz decks, but scraped off the brand name; they wrote in magic marker, and circled the insides of their Kryptonics wheels, covering the words. They all rode Independent trucks; there was no way to disguise that. Now they checked the bearings, the bolts that held on the trucks, the tension and tightness of the trucks themselves. Chris took out a wrench and loosened his; he wanted to make wide, carving turns, coming back down the hills in the darkness.

"What about Natalie?" he said.

"What about her?"

"She's not the same," he said. "I don't think so. Not like other adults. I mean, the way she talks to us, all business. She doesn't shift the tone of her voice because we're younger, she doesn't condescend, doesn't really care if we like her."

"But we never really hear her talk to other people," Kayla said.

"Still, she's different."

"You just think she's different," she said. "You want her to be."

"You don't?"

"It's not like I have a crush on her or anything."

The MAX stopped and started again, sliding past PG&E Park, all the dark empty seats, the black slant of the baseball diamond far below.

"It's been a week," Chris said. "You think we'll work for her again?"

"You know the deal," Kayla said. "I have to call her every day at the same time, and she tells me yes or no. Lately it's 'no, no, no.'"

"What else does she say?" Chris said.

"I should get the money soon," she said. "The payment for the last time. When are we going to put it away?"

The money was adding up; the three of them kept it, never spent it, stored it in their hiding place. One day they would all move away, and they would live together, somewhere, and they would live in a way that no one had lived before, a way they were still figuring out. The money was an important part of the plan. Crucial.

"Maybe she's worried because of what happened last time," Chris said.

"She doesn't even know," Kayla said. "Even Leon hardly knows."

Leon didn't seem to notice she was talking about him. He was too busy adding some scratchiti to the train's window, using a house key to mark the letters B-E-W-I- and starting on an L. The other two watched him; as he worked, he made a noise with his lips that seemed unintentional. Silver duct tape circled his shoe, holding the sole on—they were the same shoes he'd been wearing when the accident happened. Lately he seemed calmer, quieter, the set of his jaw less antagonistic than usual. He was hardly hungry at lunch, or after school; he seemed disinterested in studying. When they asked him about the accident, what had happened, what it felt like, he acted as if he could not remember it. *It didn't feel bad* was all he'd say, and that was both frustrating and tantalizing. They had difficulty believing there wasn't more he could tell them, something he was keeping back. Secrets were against the code.

"What, Leon?" Kayla said. "What are you thinking?"

"Hey," he said, looking up.

"I don't know," Chris said. "It seems like 'The Bewildered' is a good name for a band of losers, maybe, but more like the opposite of a name for people who are smart."

"And we don't need a name," Kayla said.

"Also," Chris said, "that makes us seem like people who join things."

"Joiners," Kayla said.

"It's not a name," Leon said. "I mean, saying someone is bewildered is always in comparison to what everyone else agrees makes sense, you know. So if everyone else, all the adults think you're bewildered, then you're actually not, you probably actually have a clue."

Chris looked up, out the window, at Highway 26, running parallel. A lone car, a long sedan, kept pace; suddenly, the driver opened his door—to slam it tighter or to spit something on the street—and the inside of the car was illuminated. An old man with tangled white hair, smiling to himself, driving late at night, going home or running away. He slammed his car door and the light went out, he disappeared, and in the same moment the train plunged into the tunnel, underground.

The lights flickered; something was wrong with them. Had the pointy-bearded man moved a row closer? It seemed as if he had, but it was hard to say, because now it was dark. The three sat close together, waiting; the next stop was theirs.

"Anyway," Kayla said, "don't worry, I have a plan. I'm gathering all the information we have about Natalie, in a notebook. I'm figuring how to find out where she lives, moving backward from the phone number I have for her. Then we can find out some more, find out how different she really is."

"Washington Park," said the woman's prerecorded voice from the speaker overhead. The lights returned, and the three stood, braced against each other as the train jerked to a stop.

They exited through the sliding doors. Chris looked behind them, but it didn't seem like the bearded man had followed. He'd stayed on the train, which was already gone, leaving them here, in the white tile of the tunnel.

"Holy crow," Kayla said, spitting down onto the tracks.

"I can't wait."

"Listen to you," Chris said. "Look at you. Copying. Maybe you're the one with the crush on Natalie."

"Je nai yo!" she said.

Leon was already waiting, holding the elevator door open. Now they were close, preparing themselves. Only Chris had a helmet, a skull sticker on one side; Kayla took out her leather gloves, the palms and fingers worn down, shiny. She practiced kick-flips, the sharp crack of her board's tail on the metal floor echoing off the walls. The numbers above the buttons counted the elevator's rise, the feet above sea-level. The tunnel was at 450 feet, and they climbed; the doors opened at 693 feet. They stepped out, surrounded by the zoo parking lot and the signs for the Washington Park shuttle, which didn't run this late. Lamps cast circles of light, here and there, illumination for security—exactly what they hoped to avoid.

They moved silently; they did not skate; not yet. A double thickness of ten-foot chain-link fence, with barbed wire on top, stretched up from the entrance gate a hundred feet away. The three moved closer, up to the right. Tossing their skateboards over, whispering, they went under the first fence, climbed the second—Kayla tapping the metal NO TRESPASSING sign with her fingernails—and slid down a slope of ground cover, tangled bushes. Regrouping, they climbed up through more of the same undergrowth, staying low and quiet, then pulled themselves up through the supports of a long wooden deck, and atop it, helping each other.

Here they stood, on the deck, near the mountain goats—asleep, white and shaggy, raising their bearded, horned heads at the sound of the whispered voices, the dark shapes of the three hurrying past.

"Hey, boys," Chris said, waving. "We're back."

"Quiet," Leon said.

When they reached the asphalt, they gently, quietly set down their boards. They paused for a moment, looking down the slope, the whole zoo below them. They could already smell the animals; low calls and night cries rose here and there.

"We have to remember to time it," Kayla said. Her round watch face flashed at her wrist, moonlight catching there. "How long did it take, last time?"

"Eight minutes through the zoo," Leon said. "Twenty to downtown."

With that, he was gone, out ahead, the sole of his right foot flashing—the straight stripe of duct tape, there—and then both feet on the board, his body down in a tuck, his left arm angled straight out in front and his palm facing down, his hand cutting the air and streaming it over him.

"Go ahead," Chris said to Kayla. "I'll catch up."

"Right," she said. "Try."

She pushed off and Chris followed, keeping her in sight. They went slow at first, the bumps still there, the lighter stones in the asphalt blurring together into straight lines as the warm air shifted cool and the ground went smooth. All three liked the speed, though none so well as Kayla, who could control it best. They shot across the bridge, the dull empty tracks of the miniature zoo train below, the wind in their ears, their eyes going teary. No one else did this; no one would think of it. Here was the first sharp right into an S turn—Kayla ahead leaning into it, dragging her gloved fingertips along the ground—and then the swooping left under a low arch, out past the sea lion pools and the otters, and under another arch, underground—into a cave, Chris holding his breath because it was almost like being underwater, the edges of the dark glass walls lost and the shadowy fish suspended, hanging, swimming around him and then here was the stretch of carpet under his wheels, slowing him with its friction that had to be anticipated, leaning back, Kayla already off it, and then asphalt again and his wheels loose as he shot past the elephant seals, rising so wise and fluent like huge black ghosts on a flickering white movie screen, watching, waving flippers and tails, huge enough to swallow three of him—and he was out, cool, unfishy air rushing past as he swooped around the penguin house and began to lose speed on the flats (this was a dangerous section, exposed and slow; the second time they'd done this a night watchman, some kind of security person, had run out, emerging near the Bearwalk Cafe, but by the time he got to where Kayla had been she was fifty yards past him, and he was facing the wrong way, watching her go, as Leon and Chris passed on either side, howling as they swept by, toward the gibbons) and had to start pumping hard to maintain momentum. He could hear Leon's foot, and Kayla's, their feet slapping in syncopation as they shot past the gibbons in their tall cages, up all night on manila ropes. The sound of wheels startled, roused the bears, off to the left. The air was thick with the smells of manure and hay and strange animal musks. Bamboo and ferns and cool, broad-leafed plants slipped by, slick against his bare arms. His legs ached, but the next long slope was coming, right after the Asian elephant building, and then gravity again letting loose, just enough—

—swooping down under the tall totem pole with its arms outstretched, all the frightening heads in profile, piled up, and he rocketed past the Alaskan Tundra, the slow musk ox and the hidden grizzly bear and the ragged, halfhearted gaunt wolves howling now. There was no better feeling, no name for it, no better sound, and the best was to be together, the three of them—Chris, Kayla, Leon—the points of a triangle, bending and twisting the sides, the corners and angles; he liked to be last, to keep the other two in sight, and to imagine how at the same time all the snakes were winding themselves tighter, the jaguars and tigers pacing, snapping through liquid turns like his own, and the crocodiles' slitted yellow eyes staring beneath lukewarm water, and the bad-tempered zebra, the blue-tongued giraffe turning its long neck in wonder.

They skated, their twelve wheels roaring. There was only the moon overhead, the animals above them, the city below. No one else did this; no one would think of it. And ahead Chris could see a strange light in the sky. Glaring, shining, dead ahead, calling them in. He watched as Leon, still out in front, stood up from his crouch, his body straight but his trucks wobbling, the board unsteady beneath him at that speed. Leon's head turned and his face flashed sideways in the moonlight—what was he looking at? not where he was going—and his wheels caught something or he simply lost it. His body catapulted and skidded on one side, his board kicked back, spinning so Kayla barely missed it, so Chris had to swerve around it.

Both shot by where Leon lay motionless, dark against the asphalt. Kayla leaned back, put her gloves down and slid sideways, her wheels screeching, her body only inches above the ground. Chris rode off the shoulder, leaning against the bite of the gravel, the friction, but it was too much and he was jerked loose, forward, his board lost behind him and his feet still underneath, trying to catch up before he went down, arms windmilling, feet slapping as he ran up the side of a hill, saved like a runaway truck, helmet rattling on his head, his heart and breath rattling, too, as he turned, searching back toward Leon, toward the light.

Kayla had already reached Leon, who was trying to climb a fence, to get a better view. The left side of his jeans was shredded, the sleeve of his flannel shirt completely gone. Blood there, and in the moonlight the grit visible, dark asphalt in the wound. He didn't seem to notice.

"Are you in some kind of shock?" Kayla was saying.

"What is your deal?"

She and Chris tried to climb up, to be at the same level as Leon, to talk to his face, to see what he was seeing. He didn't seem to hear them.

Highway 26, the Sunset Highway, stretched out below, a few car headlights climbing. Closer, fifty feet away from the three, a workman stood in a cherrypicker, bright floodlights fixed on him from below. The man was working on the electrical line. He wore a yellow helmet, and a black, rubber outfit, thick safety gloves. He adjusted the lines with a long-handled pole, assorted pincers and attachments on its end. The crane that held the cherry-picker aloft groaned, moving the man higher and lower when he gave hand signals. A spark kicked out, fell, disappeared. Leon clung to the fence, watching, transfixed.

"Listen," Kayla said. "We can't stay here. We'll be caught. We've got to get through the fence, over there, then down to the streets." She pointed toward the enclosure of the tree kangaroos, where the fence was bent out.

Leon looked over at her, as if awakening. He turned and smiled at Chris, then began to climb down.

"Are you all right?" Chris said. "Can you skate?"

"Of course I can skate," he said.

5.

It was not easy to pursue someone by public transportation, but if Natalie didn't call them, come to them, the three would come to her. They needed darkness, even as the days were getting longer, even if it was a school night. Things were complicated, but the three appreciated complications; they recognized them as opportunities.

"Thank you!" they called to the bus driver as they climbed out the back door. He didn't answer. He was still bent at them for practicing their music in the back of the bus; Kayla on the flute, Chris on the clarinet. It would've been even louder if Leon had taken out his trombone, but he'd refused to play. He'd just sat there with a lost, thoughtful look on his face, holding a galvanized nail between his teeth.

Now the #75 pulled away from them, the lighted windows sliding around a dark, long curve, disappearing. The three watched it go, their instruments put away, their skateboards on the ground, their packs on their backs. It smelled like trash burning somewhere, an unseen fire.

"It's down this way," Kayla said, checking the address in her notebook. "South of Johnson Creek."

Leon took the nail from his mouth and threw it into the bushes. They began to skate on the rough street, past the dark houses. Chris had new shoes—black Chuck Taylor high-tops, as always—and his mother had bought them a full size too big, so he stumbled a little when he kicked off. Leon skated better than he walked; he limped a little, lately, though claimed he didn't. A week had passed since his spill at the zoo, and under the high streetlights it looked as if his arm was still bleeding, hardly forming a scab. Leon kicked harder, away from Chris, trying to catch Kayla. She was out ahead, proud that she'd done the detective work, found the address, wanting to get there first.

The blacktop gave way gradually, the street beneath them turning to dirt. Picking up their boards, they began to walk.

"So we'll just go up to her door and knock?" Leon said. "I doubt she'll be very happy to see us."

"I just kind of want to see her house," Chris said, "you know? See if she lives with someone else or she doesn't, or if she's married, or what—"

"No way," Kayla said. "She is definitely not."

Ahead, the dark shapes of houses loomed, lights here and there.

"—and what she's doing with all that wire," Chris continued, "and everything—she never really explains, or tells us anything about herself."

"Why would she?" Kayla said. "It's not like we ever ask her anything, either."

"So, what?" Leon said, still waiting for an answer. "We'll just stroll up to her door and knock?"

Kayla swung her pack around to the front, unzipped it, and reached inside. She pulled out the orange phone headset, trailing its wires, the alligator clips on the ends.

"Hey," Leon said. "How did you get that? Did you even ask me?"

"It belongs to all of us," she said. "And I'm the only one who knows how to work it."

"You do?"

"Now I do." Kayla stopped walking and pointed straight ahead, at a low structure, all its windows flickering with bright fluorescent lights. The only neighbor was a ramshackle Victorian with all its windows boarded up.

"That's the trashiest house I've ever seen," Chris said.

"It's a trailer," Kayla said. "That doesn't really count."

"This is definitely it? Why would she live all the way out here?"

"Because she's not like other people, that's why. She doesn't want to be surrounded by them. You're the one who's always saying she's different."

"I didn't say she definitely is," Chris said. "I only said she might be."

"That's what we're finding out," Kayla said.

Nearby, under a tall cedar, Natalie's truck was parked; Kayla pointed to it as she spoke, but none of the three moved closer. They stood indecisively on the dirt road, watching the house, stealing glances at each other.

"Whatever you guys want to do," Leon said. "I'm easy."

"'I'm easy'?" Kayla said. "That phrase is disallowed."

"And start having an opinion, Leon," Chris said. He started toward the truck, closer, and the others followed. "She wouldn't go anywhere without her truck, would she?"

"She could have another car."

"But would she leave all the lights on?"

They stashed their skateboards and musical instruments under the truck and leaned close against it, for cover. Its metal sides smelled of dirt, gasoline, rust. Through the tinted window, Chris saw the familiar orange carpet, the empty back of the pickup.

"Perfect," Kayla said, her neck bent, her face looking up. She pointed to the telephone pole, rising close to the truck, next to the cedar that stretched overhead. "We're going to tap into her phone line."

"What if no one calls?"

"At least we'll be able to see better from up there."

"If she's here," Chris said.

"If this is even her house," Leon said. "Who's climbing?"

"Chris," Kayla said. "You're still hurt, and I need my hands free."

"Why?" Leon said.

"To write," she said.

"I'm fine," Leon said. "What?" But he didn't argue any further as Kayla handed the spikes and harness to Chris. She clipped the plastic phone headset to his belt and shoved a heavy screwdriver into his back pocket.

"We'll be up in the tree," she said. "Close by."

Chris began to climb. He had no gloves. The spikes slipped—still too big, despite his new shoes. As he moved slowly up the wooden pole, he listened to the metal bending on the hood, then the roof of the truck's cab; Kayla and Leon stood up there, reached for the cedar's lowest branches, and pulled themselves up, out of sight. Chris took it slow, pausing to breathe every other step; he did not look down. He felt exposed.

"What if she sees us?" he said.

"She probably wouldn't even care," Kayla said. She and Leon were above him, waiting.

"She'd only see me, anyway," Chris said. "You two, she couldn't see."

After ten minutes, his head was even with the cross-beams, near the wires. The wires cut through the branches of the tree and gouged the trunk. He kicked his feet in hard, to hold him, and leaned back against the strap, resting.

"Careful, Leon," Kayla said. "Watch your hands; the wire is right there."

"I am being careful," he said.

They sat less than ten feet away, in the branches, looking at Chris.

"What next?" he said.

Kayla pointed out the plastic box, tucked up high, among the insulators. It was gray plastic, and it wasn't locked—there was no reason anyone would be here, no reason anyone should be. Chris pried the cover away with the screwdriver, as Kayla directed, then hooked the headset's alligator clips to the stiff loops of wire she described to him. She was whispering, reading from her notebook, facts she'd copied from books and the Internet.

"Now, we wait," she said. "By the way, I got her payment, for the last time—over three hundred. We'll put it away the day after tomorrow. Sunday afternoon."

"I just wish she'd call us for a new job," Leon said. "I can climb. I'm fine."

"A little bewildered, maybe," Kayla said.

"Hilarious," Leon said. "Funny, Kayla."

"That's more like it," Chris said.

"Keep your voices down," she said. "And we still have to stash the last money. Leon, if you miss another meeting, we'll go without you. And have you been practicing that Handel? The Royal Fireworks one?"

They waited. The canvas straps were tight around Chris's hips; his legs already ached, and he picked at the splinters in his palms. It looked more comfortable in the tree. Below, oblong rectangles of light spilled out of the trailer's windows, into the ragged yard, shining on all kinds of torn-up paper. There was no movement through the windows; square reflections, mirrors or shiny books, covered the surfaces of tables and counters. That was all. Chris looked down; the ground looked distant, solid. He tried not to remember, to imagine how Leon had twisted in this same harness, sliding all the way from the top.

Suddenly, there was movement, a shadow cast, sliding inside, across the far wall, and then there was a woman, framed there, her dark brown, wavy hair around her shiny white shoulders. She wore a black bra, and perhaps nothing else; the window frame cut her off at the waist, only her torso visible.

"That's not her," Leon said.

"It is. She just dyed her hair," Kayla said.

"Why?"

"Maybe that's the real color."

"Are you sure that's her?" Chris said. The woman below looked slighter, more fragile, than Natalie.

"Look at her face," Kayla said, "and the way she's walking around, and the way she just spat in the sink."

"Right, right."

Natalie held something silver, something in tinfoil; she filled a pot with water, put it on the stove. The bra straps were straight and black against her pale skin. Dropping the foil into the water, she crossed the small room, stared out the window, and smiled.

"She can only see her own reflection," Kayla said, whispering.

"She's smiling at herself, then," Chris said.

Leon sat silent in the tree, close to where the electrical

lines stretched through the branches.

"This is great," Kayla said.

Another five minutes passed. Natalie stepped deeper into the room, so they could no longer see her. Chris glanced over at the tall, abandoned house next door—a place no one lived, but a place someone could. His legs trembled. As he tried to hold them steady, Natalie stepped into view. She took a tall glass from a cupboard; she filled it with water, mixed a spoonful of something orange into it, then drank it straight down, her head tilted back. She scratched her forehead, brushed her hair away from her eyes, and pulled it up. Her whole scalp seemed to come loose.

"Whoa," Chris said. "Did she just pull off her hair?"

"Shh," Kayla said. "It's a wig, obviously."

Natalie's hair had been shaved close to her scalp, a dark shadow on her head. She looked somewhere between a boy and a woman. Holding the wig upright, in one hand, she disappeared through a doorway. She returned, in a moment, without the wig, her head still bare. At the sink again, she splashed water on her face, and ran her hands along the crown of her head, as if reminding herself of her skull's shape. Her head looked so much smaller, unprotected. The sight of it made Chris reach up and touch his own hair, the soft bristles coming back, and to squint over at the smooth shape of Leon's head.

Natalie spun without warning, away from the sink, facing the window. The three could hear the ringing telephone from where they were; Chris was so transfixed, watching, that he didn't move until Kayla hissed at him. Hands shaking, he pulled at the plastic headset, dangling below him, and pressed it to his ear.

It was Natalie's voice—clearly hers, straight and sharp—alternating with a man's voice that was high-pitched and uncertain.

"Natalie?"

"Yes."

"It's Steven."

"Steven?"

"You know," the man said. "From San Jose. Okitonics."

"Okitonics?" she said.

"Right," he said. "Where we used to work together."

"I don't think I work there anymore."

"I know that," he said. "Neither do I."

"This was in San Jose? Holy crow. California?"

"I'm here," he said. "Here in Portland."

"How did you find me?"

"I'm living on a houseboat. Barely south of the Sellwood Bridge, down from Oaks Park—the amusement park, you know, it's just open for the season."

Chris repeated everything he could, whispering, struggling to keep up, to follow the conversation, to relay enough that Kayla could write it down. Still, he watched Natalie as he listened, as she talked on the phone. Now she was searching for a stub of pencil, then writing, it looked like, on the wall next to the phone. It was as if Chris could hear the scratching she made, because at the same time, closer, Kayla was also writing, copying down the conversation he relayed.

"Did you follow me here?" Natalie was saying.

"What? No, nothing like that. I came up here to get away for a little while. How are you?"

"Did someone tell you where I was?"

"It was a whim," the man, Steven, said. "Well, what it was, was I was in Fred Meyer this morning, shopping, and I thought I saw you, or someone who really looked like you, except your hair was different—"

"I bet," Kayla said, whispering in the tree, and the three stifled their laughter.

"—I've been curious what happened to you," Steven said. "I thought we were beginning to be friends, at the very least, and then whatever happened happened, and you were gone."

Natalie paced across her kitchen, twirling so the phone cord wound tight around her neck. Her scalp flashed in straight, white lines through the bristles of her hair. She twisted back the other way and the phone cord unwound.

"Will this reach over there?" Chris said. "I have to get off this pole. My legs are all asleep. I might fall."

"Don't drop it," Kayla said.

He swung the headset on its cord, like a pendulum— the tiny voices coming and going—and Kayla reached out and caught it. She held it to her ear, and Leon, standing on a branch beneath her, leaned his face in close. The thin cord stretched from the pole to the tree.

Chris pulled his left foot free, the spikes loose from the wood. Climbing down took less effort, but it was just as unnerving. He glanced down at Natalie, still talking on the phone, then up at Kayla and Leon, listening, not watching him or even aware that he was descending.

He jumped down the last four feet; the ground beneath him felt unsteady, yet reassuring. He unbuckled the harness, the spikes, slid them under the pickup, then crawled across the truck's hood. Through the dark windshield he saw a wire clipper, a hammer, a Slim Jim wrapper and a baseball cap on the dashboard. He kept moving, standing, pulling himself into the tree, climbing toward his friends.

Leon climbed higher, on a branch above Kayla; she slid sideways, so Chris could sit next to her on the branch.

"Yes," Kayla said. "Now things are really getting interesting." She looked at Chris, then up at Leon. "Watch your hands, Leon—the power line. Your hand's right on it."

The headset's cord still stretched to the telephone pole, the alligator clips holding. The headset was tight between Kayla's shoulder and head, and she was writing so fast that the branch shook. Chris looked down and tried to read the notebook, the piece of the conversation he'd missed. Kayla's dark pencil angled across, ignoring the lines: WATERLILY. W-A-T-E-R-L-E-L-I-E. FRIENDSHIP. ACCIDENT.

She held out the headset, her hand sticky with sap, and

Chris took it. He lifted it between their ears, so they could both listen, their faces pressed together.

"Who told you that?" Natalie was saying.

"There were all kinds of stories," Steven said. "You never came back, so no one knew what was true. I guess it was never clear to me if you left your job, or if there really was some kind of accident, or maybe both, or what—"

"Why are you so curious? Is this any of your business?"

Chris felt his face shift as Kayla smiled, eagerly listening.

"Because we were friends," Steven said to Natalie. "We are friends. I thought we were. I was just calling because I thought I saw you, and I was curious. I don't mean to—"

"Everyone looks similar in Fred Meyer," Natalie said. "It's that department store lighting in there." The pot on the stove was boiling over; she fished out the foil packet, waving it, hot, all her actions full of impatience. "I must admit I have no idea what you're getting at," she said. "Did you want to see me?"

Chris listened, Kayla's cool, soft, smooth cheek pressed against his cheek, her sweet breath like a pulse, the edge of her ear touching his ear. Leon, above them, had stretched over, his head on top of theirs, his ear pointing down so he could hear, too. The bones of their skulls formed a kind of triangle where they could hear each other swallow, feel each other blink. They all listened, simultaneously, and made sense of the words. It was as if they were reading each other's minds, a hint of how it might be, one day, between them, if they stayed true to each other, if they found their way.

"Sure, I guess so. That'd be great," Steven was saying. "Just to get together and talk. Name a time and place, and I'll be there."

6.

SWIRLS OF GASOLINE, visible even in the moonlight, colored the water of the harbor; loose packs of carp slid beneath the surface, nosing for garbage, casting new wrinkles. The cabin cruisers rocked and settled, their names painted in smug golden letters: XTASEA, JUNK BOND, THIRD WIFE.

Steven uncleated his lines and coiled them on the dock. When he started the engine, it coughed black smoke that dissipated into the dark sky. The Waterlelie was wide, and very slow, the steering wheel in the stern. He eased her away from the dock, followed the buoys out into the channel. As he steered, he watched Heather, who sat alone in the cabin, wearing dark glasses, Ross panting at her feet. The dog looked like a cross between a hyena and a German shepherd; he wore a red vest, with white letters on it that read, PLEASE DON'T PET ME I'M WORKING.

"What are you doing?" Heather called.

"Once we're out on the river," Steven said, "I'll tie

down the wheel and join you."

Heather was the coordinator of a nonprofit organization, called The Seeing Eye, that trained guide dogs. She herself was gradually losing her sight; cataracts had led to detached retinas, and numerous operations had scarred them beyond further repair. Steven had known her for just over a month, and the changing, uncertain degree of her blindness often made it a little more difficult to tell what she could or could not see. To assume too much was unkind, and to assume too little could be worse.

"We're underway?" Heather said, hearing his approach. Her face was pale, smooth and heart-shaped, her dark, curly hair swept back from a sharp widow's peak.

"Yes," Steven said. "She's thirty-six feet long, bow to stern, and indestructible." He began to describe the oak floors, the round brass plugs instead of nails, the table hanging on pulleys, the portholes.

"Can we go out on the deck?" Heather said. "It's too quiet, too still in here; I want to feel that I'm on a boat, not in a living room."

He moved the small table out onto the bow, where there was just enough space for two chairs. He set the plate of crackers and cheese there, and the bottle of wine, then helped Heather come forward.

"You look wonderful," he said, as she stood.

"All for you." She held out her arms, on display. Her hips and shoulders were full, her body strong and solid. Almost six feet, a couple inches taller than Steven, she wore red, high-heeled sandals that lifted her even higher. Her dark curls reached her shoulders, the blue and white striped shirt a little like a sailor's.

Now they were out in the current, already under the Sellwood Bridge, traveling north. Steven had set the wheel straight with a bungee cord. The river was so empty, and they were moving so slowly, that he could easily change direction in time to avoid any potential danger.

"I like the wind," Heather said. "Sometimes I can hear it in the tops of trees, or whistling around buildings, and then in a moment it crashes down on me—the more vision I lose, the more wind will affect my mood, I think. It's taking the place of the sun."

"That's beautiful," he said, pouring more wine. "Touching, I mean. We're passing Oaks Park, on the right. I guess you can hear those kids screaming. They're on the rollercoaster, the Ferris wheel. I can see the lights down below the trees, and then up above. We'll have to go there sometime."

"I've been there," Heather said, "slid down the long pink slides. Bumper cars—I shot rifles at the shooting gallery. I shot the piano players, the skunk, everything. I've been there. I've seen it."

"Sorry," Steven said. He felt Ross's cold snout against his hand; the dog was under the table.

"Don't be sorry." Heather smiled, then shifted to a more neutral expression; he knew that this was because she could not see his expression, and that the two of them were still too unfamiliar to read each other. Her lips were dark red, her wide-set eyes shadowed with pale blue as she took off her dark glasses, her eyelids lined precisely. Her eyes themselves were cloudy, half open, the pupils wandering and searching.

"Is it '*The* Waterlily,'" she said, "or just 'Waterlily'?"

"It's actually 'Waterlelie,' L-E-L-I-E," he said. "The guy I rent it from is Dutch."

"Lelie," Heather said, testing the sound.

"I'm so happy you're finally here," he said. "That you made it, I mean. I really could have picked you up, though."

"Of course not," she said, "it's good to practice with Ross on the bus—though it's going to be a while before he's properly trained. If ever."

Steven sliced more cheese, then slid the plate closer to Heather. He enjoyed watching her eat, always with her hands, searching, identifying, slowly finding a cracker. There were crumbs on her chin, all down the front of her shirt. Watching her, he could always look anywhere he wanted. Into the top of her purse, for instance; the white cane was visible—it telescoped to almost five feet long, from only twelve inches. He liked to watch her shake it out straight so it opened instantly, like a magician's trick.

"So what did you do on your day off?" Heather said.

"Nothing really," he said. "I could've worked today."

"Even volunteers need days off." Heather smiled again. "Especially volunteers."

"I cleaned the boat," he said. "Went shopping, over at Fred Meyer."

"Find some bargains?"

"Actually," he said, "no, but a kind of strange thing happened. I ran into someone I used to work with, back in San Jose, someone I didn't know was here. It surprised me."

"How so?" Heather said.

"Not that I knew her that well or anything—it wasn't anything like that," he said. "She was an acquaintance."

"It wasn't anything like *what*?" Heather said, laughing. "She must have been *some* kind of acquaintance, the way you're talking. What happened?"

"Something," he said. "She just kind of disappeared. An accident, I heard, though it was always sort of unclear, people talking. Everyone thought she'd come back, she just never did."

"And you talked to her?"

"I talked to her a lot of times," he said.

"At Fred Meyer," Heather said. "Today. That's what I meant."

"Oh," Steven said. "Today. Well, I was kind of startled, and a little unsure if it was really her. I almost did, and then I didn't, and then I missed the chance."

The table shifted as the dog stood up beneath it. His nails slipped on the deck; he barked.

"Ross!" Heather said, and instantly the dog sat down, an ashamed expression on his face.

"It's a cat," Steven said.

"On shore?"

"No, right here on the boat."

"Yours?"

"A stowaway," he said. "She lives on the dock."

The cat stood on the roof of the cabin, overhead. Black and white, she arched her bony spine, fur rising there, her tail thick and straight as she stared down at Ross.

"Still," Heather said, reaching under the table to pat the dog. "No excuse for that behavior."

Beneath the sound of the engine, a silence began to settle. Steven watched the cat disappear around the deck, toward the stern. Slowly, the boat plowed through the dark water, slipping along the west side of Ross Island. Heather tilted her head at the sound of the cars on the bridge overhead. Steven looked across the starboard side, past the green lights shining on the boat's bow. The Marquam and Hawthorne Bridges spanned the river ahead; soon he'd see the lights of the other bridges: the Morrison, Burnside, Steel, Broadway.

"I think you should call information," Heather said. "See if she has a phone number."

"What?" Steven said.

"The woman you think you saw. Let's try it now."

"Why?"

"Why not?"

"Why are you so interested?"

"I like the intrigue of it," she said. "And I want to find out why it makes you so nervous."

She had him find his cell phone in the cabin, and then—once he'd found Natalie's number—convinced him to call.

"You have to," she said. "You'll always wonder, otherwise."

He dialed the number. It rang only twice before being answered, and he wasn't certain, at first, if it was Natalie's voice. He had a difficult time explaining to her who he was, and he felt uncomfortable, awkward with Heather right there, listening.

"This was in San Jose?" Natalie said, the phone line crackling around her words. "Holy crow. California?"

"I'm here," he said. "Here in Portland."

"How did you find me?" she said. "Did you follow me here?"

"What?" he said. "No, nothing like that—" As he spoke, he turned to check the bow, the water ahead. The cat appeared, running along the gunwale, and was gone again; when Steven turned back, he saw how intently Heather was listening, her ear tilted toward him as she leaned forward to pet Ross's head.

"Accident?" Natalie was saying. "I'm not sure I believe in such a thing."

It startled him, the ease with which he'd found her, and yet the tone of her voice sounded even less familiar than when he'd first met her. Standing, he walked away from the table, back into the cabin.

"There were all kinds of stories," he said. "You never

came back, so no one knew what was true."

"Why are you so curious?" she said. "Is this any of your business?"

"Because we were friends," he said. "We are friends. I thought we were. I was just calling because I saw you, and I was curious. I don't mean to impose—"

"I must admit," Natalie said, interrupting him. "I have no idea what you're getting at. Did you want to see me?"

"Sure," he said. "I guess so. That'd be great. Just to get together and talk. Name a time and place, and I'll be there. Or come by the boat; I'll take you out on the river."

"So you're down there by the Riverside Corral?" she said, sounding more familiar again, less contentious.

"I guess so. That's near the river, right? Isn't that a strip bar?"

"Yes," she said. "Wait, hold on."

The line went silent; Steven tried, but could not hear her breathing.

"Is there a problem?"

"I thought maybe someone was outside," she said. "How about you come over next Wednesday evening? For a drink or something. I'll try to tell you how to get here."

Steven listened to Natalie's directions and wrote them down. "I'd better go," he said. "I'm really happy to have found you. I'll see you then. Great."

Both Heather and Ross looked up as Steven returned to the table.

"Weird," he said. "A voice from the past."

"That sounded like someone who was more than an acquaintance," she said. "'I'm so happy to have found you—'"

"I guess." Steven was uncertain what to say. "I mean, I spent a little time with her, together, but before we really got to know each other she kind of disappeared."

"Did you find her attractive?"

"I don't know." He tried to picture Natalie, then laughed.

"What?"

"I was just thinking of something they used to say about her. I guess she was attractive—short, energetic, with dark hair. A lot of drive. Energy."

"You already said energetic. So what did they say about her?"

"It's a little crass," Steven said. "Forget it. The thing is, she and I struck up a conversation in a hallway, by chance, and then we hung out a few times. She wasn't, isn't much older than me, but she was an executive, you know, more or less one of the founders of the company."

The cups and pans, hanging from ceiling hooks in the cabin, rang lightly together as a stray, angling wake gently stirred the boat.

"And?" Heather said. "You're making me impatient."

"The guys used to joke that she was the kind of woman who probably didn't have nipples or pubic hair— that she was cold."

"Did you find out differently?" Heather said, teasing.

"I don't know," he said. "I mean, not specifically, not those things. Not that I thought she was cold, exactly. Just businesslike."

"And she simply disappeared. And now you've found her, and you're going to get together. Very interesting. Promising."

Steven poured more wine, and they both sipped at their glasses, leaning back in their chairs as if in contemplation. Heather's hair hung down in front of her eyes and he kept expecting her to brush it away; he wanted to reach out and do it for her. Her leg rested against his, under the table, and he wondered if it were accidental.

"Where are we?" she said, her voice startling him.

"What do you mean?"

"I mean, where are we, how far have we gone?"

"We've passed under the Burnside Bridge," he said, uncertain how detailed to make his description. Ross watched him from under the table, looking on as if daring him to exaggerate or stray. "The whole city's on our left," Steven continued, "downtown, all the buildings lit up, the lights of the houses on the hill behind it. You can see a lot from the water. We could come back in a few weeks, for the Fourth of July fireworks—"

"I'd like that," she said. "I like the sounds, imagining them against the sky. Last year was the first time I couldn't see them at all." She bent her neck as if looking up into the sky. "You find me attractive," she said. It was not a question. "Would you be attracted to me if I were gaining vision, instead of losing it?"

"I don't know what you want me to say," he said.

"What you feel."

"Well," he said. "That's pretty hypothetical. Maybe not—you are the way you are."

"Fair enough," she said.

Steven couldn't tell where she was going, if she was making fun of him; he couldn't read her tone.

"You think blond women resent the gentlemen who prefer them?" she said. "Or big breasted women hate their followers?"

"Maybe they do," he said. "That's different, that's not inside."

"Are you sure it's so different?"

Steven reached out and took hold of Heather's hand, across the table. Her fingers were sticky with cheese.

"You find me attractive," he said, but it sounded more like a question than he'd meant it to.

"I don't know," she said. "What do you look like?"

"I could describe myself," he said.

"No," she said. "Don't."

She took back her hand and hit a button on her watch; a tiny, robotic voice said that it was nine twenty-eight. They would have to turn around soon.

"I read in this book," Steven said, "where a guy divided his friends into those he'd known before he lost his sight, who had faces in his memory, and those—"

"This is not about books," she said. "This is about you

and me. I have my own idea of what you look like; that's enough."

"And how do I look?"

"It's funny," she said, "but you look a lot like me. Shorter hair, but dark and thick, with eyebrows you should probably tweeze. Your breasts are smaller than mine, of course. You sometimes wear a mustache, in the winter."

"You want to know if you're close?"

"I do know some things," she said. "I can make out shapes, sometimes, in bright light. I know the way you arch your back when you laugh, for instance. Your posture worries me a little, the tentative way you move, but I might forget that. I'll believe it will change. The main thing is that the dogs like you, they trust you; they don't lie."

Dogs had always liked him, had always been eager to be near him. This was true, and it embarrassed him, and he mistrusted it even as he was willing to take credit for whatever their devotion suggested. And his appearance, he knew, was far from how Heather had imagined it. When she touched him, if she touched him—it would not be tonight, he could tell, he would be patient—she would realize that his reddish hair was thinning, that he was skinny, not strong. He wasn't proud of his body, all the pale skin, covered in freckles. He'd been told they'd grow lighter as he aged, but they hadn't. Perhaps he would tell her about them; perhaps she'd be able to feel them.

"Forest Park," he said, looking across the water, to the west.

"Largest urban wilderness in America," Heather said, intoning the phrase. "Wolves, bears, all kinds of danger."

"Still?" he said.

"I used to hike all through there," she said.

"Even in the darkness," he said, "you can see the different shades of green, the distances and heights, the different kinds of trees."

7.

TWO SETS OF HEADPHONES were attached to Kayla's Walkman
—she'd spliced the wires—and she and Chris walked close
together, listening to Mussorgsky's *Pictures at an Exhibition.*
They hurried through the last neighborhood, up the hill of
Thurman Street, toward the entrance of Forest Park, where
the trees rose solid and green, awaiting them. The day was
hot, but the sky was dark, the clouds low.

The symphony swooped, rose and fell. Chris looked
down, at the frayed cuffs of Kayla's black Dickies, the
pants' legs cut off above the ankles. He knew that she was
listening for the flute parts; he waited for the clarinets. It
all sounded eerie, like the music from a haunted house; he
knew it was supposed to be about looking at different
paintings, to capture that in music, and as he listened the
scene around him—the houses painted blue and green,
the bright red of a parked car—also seemed to fit the swell
of sound. He sucked on a butterscotch, walking, listening

closely. There, the clarinets. Chris looked ahead again, to the dark green of the trees above, then behind them. He wondered if they should have waited longer, if Leon would have shown at the meeting place, if perhaps he was there now.

The music stopped. Kayla's finger rested on the button. She pulled her headphones down around her neck, then reached out for his, then wound up the cords and put the whole thing in her pack. She looked up, into Chris's face.

"He completely forgot," she said. "Or he's doing something else."

"I don't know what it is," Chris said. "What his deal is, lately."

"A zombie," Kayla said. "It's got to be puberty or something. He's bound to come to life. Leon. He'll just get a look at himself, and then he'll get straight."

They weren't carrying their instruments, not even skateboards. This was a simple mission, a responsibility they'd put off too long. It was the money, which was now in Kayla's pack, and which they would now deposit. Not in a bank, since they all agreed a bank would suspect them, having so much money, but in their hiding place, high in Forest Park. The money always came to Kayla—cash in the mail, inside a security envelope. Never a check, never a note, never a return envelope. Just as Kayla had to be the one to call Natalie, she always received the payment. There could be no variation.

Chris held the butterscotch between his teeth for a moment, and Kayla snatched the candy in her fingers. She popped it in her own mouth, laughing, then spit it into her hand and put it back in his mouth. It tasted slightly different to him, the warm sweet stickiness now more slippery and rich.

It was only early afternoon; maybe they'd catch up with Leon, later. They had reached the end of the road, the parking lot before the trail. A Volkswagen van was parked there; it looked like it had not moved in quite some time. Orange, with dirty yellow curtains pulled across the windows, the roof popped up. A bumper sticker read, BEER: HELPING WHITE PEOPLE DANCE FOR 2,000 YEARS.

"Hippies," Chris said.

"Pathetic," said Kayla.

On the trees all around the lot, lost dog signs were tacked. Xeroxed photos of terriers, mutts, collies and labs, all pictured in their domesticated days—sitting on couches, in trucks, sometimes with children, or in knit sweaters, their tongues hanging out, their names (BUTCH, RANGER, SERENA, SHAGGY) written underneath. Every time there were more dogs, different ones. Leon's theory was that Forest Park was full of these dogs, gone feral, running together, mixing with wolves and mountain lions.

"The pack grows," Kayla said.

"You'd think, seeing all these dogs already lost, that people wouldn't bring theirs here," Chris said, "or they'd bring a leash or something."

Far off to one side, closer to the path, was a different poster. A photograph. A man with deep-set eyes and a narrow face stared out at them. His black beard ended in a sharp point, his chin like a dagger. The words stretched down the left hand side of the poster:

Victor Elias MACHADO
Legal Status:
On Post Prison Supervision for Attempted
Sex Abuse I – Expires 03/08/03

SPECIAL CONDITIONS:
Machado shall have no contact with minor
males or females nor frequent any place where
minors are likely to congregate (e.g. play-
grounds, school grounds, arcades, public parks).
Shall submit to random polygraph testing.
Shall have no contact with victim or victim's
family. Shall not use intoxicating beverages.
Shall not own/operate motor vehicles.

TARGET VICTIMS:
Minor Males or females, known or unknown to him.
REPORT ANY MISCONDUCT OR VIOLATION
TO: MULTNOMAH COUNTY COMMUNITY
CORRECTIONS

"Victor Machado," Chris said. "Sketchy. He looks kind of familiar."

"I guess that's not his van," Kayla said.

"He's probably running with the dog pack."

"On all fours?" she said. "He looks like he could. Let's go."

The path was gravel, and for a few minutes there was only the sound of their four feet, all in Chuck Taylor high-tops, scuffing along, climbing. As they climbed, it was as if the foliage closed around them. The thorned stalks of blackberry bushes snaked across the path, dark green, and above them the thick ivy, the pine trees up higher. Ferns grew on the steepest hills; on rainy days, the water passed from one plant to the next, swaying, making it look like a green waterfall. Chris had seen it. Now, though, there was no rain; the air was hot, thick, and the only breeze was high in the trees, unreachable.

"We should have brought something to drink," he said.

Kayla swung her pack around front, still looped over her shoulder, not slowing her pace. She unzipped it and reached in, but what she brought out was not a bottle of water, as he'd hoped. Instead, it was a piece of paper, creased and old and folded, the edges torn. She handed it over without a word.

It was a page from a magazine; Chris unfolded it. He glanced at the picture, then looked away, wondering if Kayla was somehow testing him. The image stayed in his mind: a naked woman, standing in a washtub, outside somewhere. Her round, heavy breasts hanging down and jutting out, one leg bent up, the other in the water, the hair between them. She stood next to a tree, maybe a tent. She squeezed a washcloth so clean water ran down her naked body; from her expression, the water was either very cold or very hot; her head was tilted back, her mouth half open. Across her tanned stomach, numbers had been written in pencil. Chris turned the paper over, to see if it was something else he was supposed to see, and there were two pictures of the same woman, naked except for black and yellow striped knee-socks; she was stretched out on a black and red wool blanket on her back and on her stomach, her face looking up. Her fingernails were long and curved, wicked. Dark red.

"You can look at it as long as you want," Kayla said. "But you can't keep it."

"What would I want with it?" Chris said.

"Don't act like you don't like it—you can barely walk and look at it at the same time, your mouth hanging open. You'll bite off your tongue."

"You're the one carrying it around," he said.

He handed it back to her, and she folded it carefully, put it away. They followed the winding path, silent again.

"Whoa," Kayla said, her arm across his chest, her finger pointing into a small canyon below. Through the trees, slanted sections of blue were visible. Chris bent down and could see a rounded edge, shimmering in the sun.

"It's a pool!" she said. "A pond."

"I've never seen it before," he said.

"We'll swim, after."

"I don't know."

"It's not like anyone's around," she said. "You can keep

your underwear on, if you want—just think how good it will feel."

"It's probably fenced off."

"As if that would stop us. Come on." Kayla looked around, finding a landmark, so she would not forget, and they resumed their climb, she rebraiding one side of her hair, tightening the rubber band around and around the tip. She almost stepped on a six-inch banana slug, but stepped sideways at the last minute.

"I'm thinking of shaving my head," she said. "That way I'll be like you and Leon."

"Like Natalie, too," he said. "Are you serious?"

"Maybe."

"What were those numbers?" he said.

"Numbers?"

"On that picture you showed me."

"Aha," she said. "You did like it."

"There were penciled numbers on it."

"Natalie's phone number."

"Why?" he said.

"She gave it to me, the first time I met her. That picture."

"But you never told us that!"

"So what?" she said. "Does it matter?"

Chris didn't answer; he walked half a step behind her, confused. He tried to check her expression without turning his head, but she didn't give anything away, only kept walking, her white T-shirt lined by the pack's straps. He could see the lines of her bra under her shirt. She'd been wearing one for more than two years now.

They passed the first *X*, carved into a tree trunk, then the second—these were false markers before the third, which was better hidden. Here, they checked to see that no one was watching, then lifted the blackberry bushes at the edge of the path, exposing a kind of tunnel through the thorns. Chris ducked down and went in first, on his hands and knees, collecting all the spiderwebs across his face, trying not to let the shoots and branches snap back to slash at Kayla. The ground angled sharply upward, but the tunnel was not long; it opened up, and they emerged into the mouth of a low, limestone cave. The opening was jagged, six feet across, three feet high, hidden by bushes.

Chris moved over, making room for Kayla. The cave was large enough for all three of them, barely. Behind them, the wall dropped down so the opening was only twelve inches high and stretched back farther than they could see. The three had decided that bats lived there.

Kayla scraped at the ground, the dirt and loose leaves, until she uncovered a flat, white rock. She lifted this, then took out the bank—a small wooden barrel, with brass rings around it, wrapped in two plastic bags. She unwrapped it and began pushing the money inside.

"How much do we have, all together, do you think?" Chris said.

"Over a thousand, easy."

"How much do we need?"

"A lot more."

"Just the three of us, living together, however we want." Chris leaned forward; through the leaves and branches of the bushes he could see a sliver of the sunlit path, thirty feet below. "That's still what we're doing, right?"

"Of course," Kayla said. "What else would we do?"

"I don't know. It's just that I haven't heard Leon say anything about it for a long time."

"Well, that's Leon. He just has some issues, like I said. It has to be a temporary thing, you know? I just hope he's not messing up at school."

"Definitely temporary." Chris watched her replacing the bank, the stone, covering it up as if nothing were there. "At least it's almost summer vacation, and most of the grades are already in. Teachers are so lazy—they just want to feed us candy, show us movies for the next two weeks."

"Right," Kayla said. "By the way, did the Honor Society tell you they might kick us out if we don't go to meetings?"

"So what?" he said. "They can't change our grades, or know what we know. They just like to have us there where they can see what we're doing."

"They want us to care what they think," Kayla said, smiling. From her unzipped pack, she took out her notebook. She opened it for a moment and pointed to a line, a date and time.

"Two days until that guy visits Natalie," she said. "Her old friend. It'll be great to see. Leon better not miss that."

Getting down from the cave was easier; they only had to be careful that no one was around to see them emerge, and then they stood, on the path again, brushing thorns and dirt from their clothes. Watching Kayla, Chris remembered about the swimming. The thought made him anxious; maybe she had forgotten. They walked. Down below, through the trees, he glimpsed the river—a few small boats, and the bridges forking, angled across the water like spokes on a wheel.

They turned a corner and could see an old woman on a mountain bike approaching, climbing, her frizzy hair escaping all around her helmet. She was barely moving; they could hear her panting, twenty feet away.

"Howdy," she said, lurching toward them.

"Howdy," they both said, rolling their eyes as soon as she was past.

Down below, closer, the railyard stretched, and the ships at the docks, the huge metal cranes bent over the river.

"Here," Kayla said. "I bet this little trail goes down to that pond."

Chris followed her, watching the zigzag part in her hair, her pack swinging from side to side across her sharp shoulders. He did not know if he wanted to swim, if he wanted to take off his clothes with Kayla, even down to his underwear. He had a feeling that something was going to happen, and he wished he knew what it was. Below, he could see the round pond, the water flat and cool and no doubt refreshing, and then it was hidden again by the trees.

"Are you sweating?" Kayla said. "I am."

"Howdy," he said, and they both laughed.

Chris bent his neck to look up through the thick branches, squinting at the now-blue sky, and in that moment Kayla stopped, and he slammed into her; they both almost fell over.

"Look," she said.

In the middle of the dirt path was a perfect little rabbit, dead. It was brown, without a mark on it, as if asleep. Kayla touched its ear with a twig, then picked up the little rabbit in her bare hands and set it down under a bush, off the trail.

"It weighs like nothing," she said. "Come on—we're close, now."

Chris hurried after her. The notebook and whatever else was in her pack jostled, keys and coins ringing. But when they'd almost reached the bottom, the level of the pond, something strange had happened. Through the trees, the blue water seemed solid, a vertical wall, as if the pond had been frozen in a cylinder, or encased in glass.

Kayla and Chris stepped into a small clearing, through tall, dry grass. The pond was not a pond at all; it was a water tank, painted pale blue, thirty feet tall, at least, with a ladder ten feet up. Round, with a flat top—that's what they'd seen from above. The ladder's bottom end was out of reach, yet a frayed rope dangled from the lowest rung. A sign on the side read, MAYFAIR RESERVOIR #1. Chris knocked his fist against the tank; he expected a hollow ringing, but there was no echo. It was like knocking on a brick wall.

Kayla smiled, batting at the hanging rope so the heavy knot swung back and forth. Before they even said a word, she took hold of it and was climbing, the soles of her shoes against the tank's metal side. Once she got to the ladder, Chris reached up and took the rope, following.

She was walking around the edge by the time he reached the top. Here, there were the remains of a campfire, a piece of foam camping mattress, a broken metal folding chair. The metal burned the palms of his hands as he pushed himself up and felt hot through the soles of his shoes; the surface was mostly clean, but marked with darker circles, where puddles had evaporated away. Graffiti read, *JUANITA + RAY* and FEAR, along with a few scattered warnings, promises.

Kayla laughed. She straightened her arms behind her and her pack dropped off, next to her feet. She danced away, pretending to swim with her arms, as if they were underwater. Chris joined her—they bumped into each other, splashed at the air, laughing, balancing close to the edge, the heat coming from above and below. One braid came loose, and Kayla's hair exploded wild on that side; still swimming, she crossed her arms in front of her, gripped the hem of her T-shirt, and pulled it over her head, threw it off so it disappeared far below. Chris swum to the edge, saw it white in the tall grass, and then turned back to the whiteness of her bra, and Kayla closer, wind-milling her arms through the air. When she reached him, her arms slowed, and her hands were at the side of her head, gripping tightly, her face close to his. He smelled her sweet shampoo, her sweat.

"You're keeping all your clothes on?" she said, pulling at his T-shirt. "They'll get wet."

Chris took off his shirt, following her. His body, he knew, looked pretty much like hers. Now she was bending down to untie her shoes. She kicked them off, unsnapped her pants. Unzipping them, she looked up at him, staring until he began to untie his shoes.

He tried to catch up and stumbled, his pants tangled around his ankles—and then he was loose, dancing, swimming with Kayla, trying not to look at her, trying to look at her. He hadn't seen her take off her bra, but she had and now her small breasts were there, amazing, moving side to side, up and down, as she leapt.

"My feet!" she said.

The metal was too hot, burning the soles of their feet—they couldn't stay airborne long enough. Hopping, they pulled on their shoes, and kept swimming, wearing only underwear and high-tops, laces whipping loose. Chris watched Kayla, the blue sky behind her, the green trees, her panties the same color as the sky. He reached out, his hand sliding across her back, low, and her arm slapped hot across his shoulder.

"Tighty-whities!" she said, laughing, pointing where the front of his briefs stuck out. Next, she picked up his shirt, spread it across the piece of foam rubber.

"Sit down," she said. "Lay back."

He smelled the dirt, the old rain caught in the foam. Kayla's small breasts looked pale and smooth, as if they'd be cool to the touch. Her nipples were dark; one stuck out and one was inverted, pushed in. He touched her spine, his finger sliding down the vertebrae. Her shoulder brushed his face as she lay back, her sour skin against his mouth for a moment. They did not talk; they did not know what to say, what they would do. Stretched out in the sun, their skin was hottest where it pressed together—the side of his knee against her thigh, her smooth calf resting over his, her nipple barely touching his arm. Leaning toward him, she held her hand over his briefs; his dick was hard, and she touched it, through the fabric. She pushed it down, let go, and it bounced back up.

"We shouldn't be doing this," she said.

"We're not doing anything," he said. "Not yet."

"We almost are."

"But we still aren't. That's the difference. We won't, will we?" Chris said. His elbow was off the foam, and the metal burned his skin. He stared past Kayla, into the sky, and listened to the wind in the trees. Closing his eyes, he still listened, and the sun shone bright, a rosy glow through his eyelids. He held out his hand and could see it without opening his eyes, the dark shadows of his fingers.

"I thought we all decided," Kayla said. "With Leon, we all agreed."

"It's more like an experiment," he said. "A test."

"But we still shouldn't tell him; we shouldn't talk about it."

"That would be a secret," Chris said. "Keeping a secret from him."

"Maybe only for a little while," she said, "until he's more like himself again. And we're not doing anything, anyway."

Chris opened his eyes. Kayla was sitting up, her bra on backward, loose around her waist; she did the clasp, spun it around, pulled it up. Her breasts were gone. She bent her elbows, straightened her arms. He reached out and touched her back again, but she leaned away from him. She laced her shoes, then stood and pulled on her pants over them; retrieving her pack, she walked toward the ladder. A few steps down, she paused, facing him.

"So you won't say anything, right?"

"All right," he said.

Her head disappeared, sinking away. There was only the empty space where the ladder surfaced, the green of the distant trees, the bushes below. And then her head reappeared, the hair still loose on one side, pulled into its braid on the other. She smiled.

"Hurry up," she said. "Do I have to tie your shoelaces for you, or what?"

8.

WAS HE LATE? The car's clock was broken, and Steven had
forgotten his watch, his wrist bare. He drove slowly,
squinting to read the numbers on the houses he passed,
then pulled over and turned on the overhead light and
checked the address again. The numbers were counting
down, and he was going in the right direction, but it
seemed unlikely that anyone lived farther down this road.
He switched the light back off, shifted his Corolla into
drive, and kept on into the darkness.

A broken-down Victorian loomed, its windows all
boarded up, and then around the other side a trailer
appeared, all its windows ablaze. The number on the
trailer matched the one Natalie had given him, but it
seemed impossible—a tree branch had fallen on the roof,
and the whole thing seemed to tilt, propped on cinderblocks; the rusted pickup out front was not the Lexus
he'd expected, that Natalie used to drive. Still, he parked.

He stepped close to the fence without opening the gate. A dog chain stretched empty, like a snake across the tangled yard; scraps of paper, torn magazines, were everywhere. And then there was movement, a shadow across the ground, and a woman moving unhurriedly inside the trailer. She walked with her head cocked, as if she'd heard his car, her hands out as if feeling her way along. It wasn't Natalie—yes, it was. He opened the broken gate in the chain-link fence, not taking his eyes off her. Her hair was long and straight, strawberry blond, different than the dark bob she used to wear, and also different than the black-haired woman he'd seen in Fred Meyer.

Halfway to the front door, he kicked a piece of paper into the air, then bent to pick it up. Natalie's face appeared in the window next to the door, leaning close, failing to see him.

"Who is it?" she called.

"Steven."

"Who?"

"You asked me to come by tonight. I might be a little late."

"Oh, Steven!" she said. "Right! That sounds familiar."

She opened the door and stood in the gap with her hand on the knob, not stepping aside or inviting him in. Barefoot, she wore a chambray work shirt and dark pants that had been roughly cut off at the ankle, rather than properly hemmed.

"Nice neighborhood," he said.

"Not really," she said, "but I like it. It's quiet."

"Didn't Gary Gilmore used to live around here?"

"Who?"

"The murderer."

"Probably." She smiled, and looked around, as if wondering what he wanted. She clearly had not been expecting him.

"Do I look different?" he said. "Maybe I had more hair." He felt his head, self-conscious. "Your hair's different, too," he said.

"Yes," she said. "Probably."

"Of course," he said, "it hasn't even been a year since we've seen each other."

Natalie walked away from him, her back turned, the door still open. After a pause, he stepped inside, closed the door, and followed. The floor in the entryway was torn yellow linoleum, showing the black and white checks beneath, the trailer seemed to shift with his every step, an unsteadiness that might be solved by a two-by-four or a folded-over piece of cardboard between the cinderblocks outside. Inside, it smelled musty, mildewed. Cold fluorescent lights hummed, illuminating everything. He looked down at the piece of magazine in his hand and saw that the page was the color of skin, with black lace along one edge. He jammed it in his pocket before Natalie noticed.

She now stood in the kitchen, in the space between a counter and the refrigerator, facing him, waiting. On the other side of the counter was a rickety table, three chrome and vinyl chairs, a ragged brown couch. Every surface reflected color, shining from the stacks of magazines that covered every surface, from the faded covers, the title atop each one the same, PLAYBOY, just in different colors. Natalie watched him looking over the magazines. She swung open the refrigerator; inside, it was almost entirely empty. A jar wrapped in tinfoil, a row of batteries, half a bottle of green Gatorade.

"I'd like to give you something to drink," she said. "Gatorade? I could mix you up some Tang, if that's more to your liking."

"Gatorade's fine," he said. As she poured a glass, he looked around again, wondering what had become of all her modern furniture, all the things she'd collected for her place in San Francisco.

"Now, why are you here?" she said.

"To visit," he said. "To catch up, you know. If tonight's not good—"

"It's perfect," she said, waving at him. "Sit down, sit down."

There was no place to sit, the chairs stacked high with magazines; he picked up a pile, moved them to the floor, and sat at the table, which was covered by six inches of PLAYBOYS; the issue in front of him was from July 1976. A brunette held a huge flag, her nude body faintly visible through a thin white dress. Happy Birthday, America! the cover said. Was the woman supposed to be Betsy Ross?

Natalie handed him the Gatorade, and he took a drink, watery and achingly cold, sweet and salty at once.

She returned to the sink and began to mix herself a glass of Tang. The spoon rang against the insides of the glass; that was the only sound, and then silence rose up. She seemed so calm, so at ease, as if none of this would be unexpected, as if it all followed from how she had been when he knew her before.

"Did you sell your place in Frisco?" he said.

Natalie just smiled, blowing on the Tang as if it were hot. Behind her, he noticed that the faceplates had been taken off all the light switches and electrical outlets, the insulation stripped to expose bare wire. He heard crickets outside, in the silence, the chirping coming and going in waves.

"You got out of San Francisco at a good time," he said. "The whole industry, I mean. The stock options were probably amazing. Did you cash out?"

"Pardon me?"

"It must have taken some work to just disappear like that."

Natalie tossed the spoon into the sink and it rattled, startling him. She leaned forward with her elbows on the counter. Her hair fell down over her eyes and she blew it away, her lower lip jutting out.

"That's none of my business, really," he said. "Sorry. That's just what I heard."

"This one's my bedroom," she said, pointing to one of the two closed doors down a hallway. "That one's my workroom, but I can't let you in there."

Steven began to set his glass on the magazine in front of him, then hesitated. He looked down at the woman and the flag and blushed.

"Don't be ashamed," Natalie said.

"I'm not," he said.

"Yes, you are. Go ahead, look all you want. I do." Natalie came around the counter and reached across the table; she flipped open the magazine in front of him and paged through it. There were ads for cigarettes and eight-track players, then the centerfold—a naked woman in feathered hair and arched eyebrows, holding a thick rope and wearing high, striped socks.

"Deborah Borkman doesn't like the meat market singles scene of L.A." Natalie said, "since sex, to her, is a private matter; but if she relates to someone on a mental level, then the physical part just follows naturally."

"What?"

Natalie kept turning the pages. There were more pages of writing, and more pictures. A pictorial of a woman and man—it was a young, bearded Kris Kristofferson, Steven realized—in a brass bed, on blue sheets, unclothed.

Natalie was standing up straight on the other side of the table, the orange glass of Tang in her hand. With her free hand, she brushed her long hair from her face.

"Listen," Steven said, "I just have to say something, and I don't want you to take it the wrong way."

"Go ahead."

"Something's weird," he said. "All I'm saying is I don't

know if you're putting me on somehow or what. All your directions are based on strip clubs—the Corral, the Acropolis—"

"That's a steak place, too," she said.

"It's different than how you were," he said, "and then all this porn lying around."

"How I was is how I was," she said. "I just can't hardly remember it. There was a transition. And I wouldn't call this pornography—pornography is more like simulated penetration, all that."

Steven looked down at Kris Kristofferson's bare ass, the woman's thin legs wrapped around his waist. Glancing away, trying to think, Steven looked at the other magazines and realized that many were duplicates, and that all of them seemed dated. The covers mentioned celebrities like Joe Namath, Billy Carter, O.J. Simpson, Lily Tomlin. Many were torn and weathered, scalloped as if left out in the rain and then dried.

"You don't think it objectifies women?" he said, finally, falling back on something he'd heard.

Natalie hardly seemed to be listening. "All the girls look like weight lifters, now," she said, "I can't even stand to look at them. They have personal trainers, and airbrushing. I like to see pores, veins, razor stubble, you know." She stretched her arms over her head, her hands almost reaching the water-stained ceiling. "And I just think back to when I was a girl, and I found these magazines, the first time—"

"In Denver?" he said. "Isn't that where you grew up?"

"One of my clearest memories is finding them, when I was a girl, in the Bicentennial. I looked at them and I felt like my body would arrive and just force the clothes right off, like it couldn't be contained. And then I'd be a person, truly at liberty—as free as they were."

"As who were?" Steven said, and then realized she meant the women in the photographs and couldn't figure out what to say next. He decided to play along, to show her he could. Glancing at the open magazine again, he gestured toward the image.

"I used to be a Kris Kristofferson fan," he said, struggling to keep his voice steady. He felt a line of sweat run down his back, under his shirt. "'Me and Bobby McGee,' all that."

"What?" Natalie said. "Who's that?"

"I just liked his singing, his songwriting. And he was an actor. A Rhodes scholar, even. Once, in an interview I read, he said that you shouldn't sleep with anyone who's crazier than you."

Natalie smiled. "So whoever you sleep with, then, is breaking that rule?"

"That's the problem, I guess."

"Did we ever sleep together?" she said.

"Why would you ask that?" he said, startled. "We were friends; I thought we were going to maybe be good friends, at least—"

"So we didn't," she said.

"Right."

She smiled and walked back around the counter. She leaned against the sink, facing him, and rolled up the sleeve of her work shirt, revealing her wiry forearm.

"So," she said. "What else do you like?"

Suddenly Steven became aware of the blackness of the windows, only reflecting the trailer's inside, and he remembered how clearly he had seen her, from outside. There were no blinds to close, no curtains to draw.

"Did you hear something?" he said.

"I was waiting to hear what you were going to say next."

"What?"

"About what you like."

"Oh," he said. "What do I like?" His neck was sore from keeping his head rigid, his vision above the open magazine in front of him. He wanted to close the pages, but he couldn't. Natalie sat down across from him, gently kicking his legs under the table, settling, her face all anticipation.

"I like the fall," he said. "The autumn. When people pile up the leaves in the streets."

"So you're saying you're a man of simple pleasures, then? Or that's how you'd like me to see you?"

"You can see me however you want."

"Tell me," she said. "I wonder about you. You want to know all about me, but what are you doing, I wonder."

"Nothing really," he said. "Taking a couple months off,

like I said, living on a houseboat, doing a little volunteer work—"

"And we knew each other before," she said. "In San Jose. Did you follow me here?"

"No. You've asked me that already—I mean, I'm glad that you turned out to be here, it's a nice coincidence, but I didn't know."

"Are you really glad? Why?"

"What?"

"Tell me about your work," she said. "Your 'volunteer work.'"

"It's for a nonprofit," he said. "An organization that helps the blind."

"And that's interesting?"

"I like it," he said. "I feel like I'm doing something worthwhile, and it is interesting—I was just reading an essay by Borges all about his friendship with the color yellow. It was very touching—"

"I'm sure it was," she said.

"Portland's a good city for blind people," he said. "The rain, it makes the world more audible, reflective; it reveals the edges of things. Snow, you know, that's like the blind person's fog—it dampens all the vibrations—"

"Yes," Natalie said. "It is a good city; I think so."

"How did you end up here?" he said. "After you disappeared, after you left California, I kept thinking I'd hear from you, but I never did."

"Sorry to disappoint you."

"What did happen? I heard lots of things."

"Really?" she said, and laughed. "To be honest, I'm more interested in what you heard. Why don't you tell me some these stories that you keep mentioning?" She tilted back her head, her eyelids half-closed, as if daring him.

"I heard you bugged out," he said, "that you'd had it, that you just didn't come back from lunch one day, cashed in your stock, didn't even warn your secretary."

"Mysterious," she said. "I like it."

"And then I also heard that what it was was that you were down in the control rooms, where the tunnels and cables intersected, where you had no reason to be, and there was some kind of short, an outage. A technician found you there. The company hushed it up, and a lot of people thought you'd be back, eventually, were expecting you to be—and some even said you were still working for the company, but on something so secret or illegal that you pretended to leave, but really didn't, or that you had to disappear."

"A likely story," Natalie said. "And what else?"

"That's about it," he said. "All I heard. Which one is closest? The first?"

Natalie looked behind her, then all around the room before fixing her gaze on him again. "I'm here now," she said. "I'm happy. It doesn't seem like there's any point in looking backward."

"But here you are," he said, slightly exasperated, "collecting old magazines, surrounded by all this exposed wiring, in Gary Gilmore's neighborhood. Something happened."

Natalie saw where he was looking. "That," she said. "That's just a hobby. I've figured out how to rewire things, and how to turn back the meters. Kilowatt hours are a whole different kind of time—"

"Be serious," he said. "I was worried. Are you serious? What are you even talking about?"

"Take it easy," she said. "Let's just talk."

"That's what I'm trying to do."

"Not so serious, though. We can talk without 'having a talk.'"

Steven looked away from her, his eyes skittering along the shiny surfaces of the magazines, the light reflecting. He wondered if it was unusually bright in the room, or if he were especially sensitive. He felt exposed.

"That's more like it," Natalie said.

He realized that he was absentmindedly turning the pages in front of him, and this time he refused to let her embarrass him. If this was what she wanted to talk about, then he would talk about it.

"That was a good time for cars," he said, turning pages. "I was like nine or ten, back then, dreaming of owning a Scirocco."

"Don't pretend like you're reading the articles! Just try—"

Standing again, Natalie began stretching her arms all over the table, snapping back the covers of different issues, unfolding centerfolds. "Look at that string bikini tan line," she said. "And here's Karen Hafter—look at her hips, amazing; no one's curvy like that anymore—and Patti McGuire; she was Playmate of the Year, you know. You can see why. She says she admires people who don't admire anybody. Look here at Daina House, Steven. She's not shy!"

Steven glimpsed white lace, a grass hut, gold sandals, a straw hat on a barn floor, military dog tags, a pinball machine, tall lizard-skin boots. He focused on the women's clothes, the things around them; looking at their bodies made him anxious.

"These women probably have daughters this old, now," he said. "I wonder where they are."

"I just want them to be how they were," she said, "the way they are, how I first saw them."

Steven paged past the centerfold, through an article about Bobby Kennedy's assassination, past a racy cartoon about George Washington and Betsy Ross. He was in the Kris Kristofferson pictorial again; he could not hurry through. Natalie was watching him.

"I see what this is now," he said. "It's from a movie."

"A pornographic movie?" she said. He could hear her smile.

"No," he said. "It's based on a book I read. Mishima. The Sailor Who Fell from Grace with the Sea. I wonder if the movie's any good—I see they moved it from Japan to England."

"That guy doesn't look very Japanese," Natalie said. "He looks more like he's in pain."

The woman in the picture was astride Kristofferson, leaning back, pulling on his hair. He grimaced, his eyes closed.

"And what happens?" Natalie said.

"You'll have to read the book," he said, "or see the movie."

"Look at how dark her nipples are; they might have rouged them."

"It's a short novel," Steven said. "It's about this group of school kids who live by their own code and have all kinds of sadistic adventures. The sailor gets involved with one of these boys' mother, a widow. That's what we're seeing here." He turned the page; the woman was standing on the bed, her crotch in Kristofferson's face.

"'Involved,'" Natalie said. "I'll say. And then what happens?"

"In the end, they trick the sailor, the kids do. They poison him."

"They kill him?"

"Anyway," he said, "I bet the movie's not that good. I've never heard of it. I don't even know if Kris Kristofferson is still alive."

Natalie abruptly stood up from the table, knocking it with her thighs; a few magazines slid off, onto the floor.

"Natalie?" he said, but her back was turned, unreadable. She opened one of the doors in the hallway, disappeared through it, closed it behind her.

Left in her wake, Steven tried to think back through what he'd been saying. He closed the magazine in front of him; the back cover was an ad for Carlton cigarettes. From where he sat, he could see down the hallway. He couldn't remember which door was which.

And then one of the doors opened and Natalie stepped out long enough to open the other door and disappear again, into the other room. After a moment, she appeared again and then began going back and forth between the rooms, carrying things: a standing mirror in a wooden frame, it looked like; a lamp with cut glass beads hanging from the shade, a high-backed wicker chair.

"Do you want a hand?" he said.

"Stay," she said, not looking in his direction.

He couldn't tell if she meant for him not to bother her or not to leave. Perhaps he should leave, though she hadn't exactly asked him to. He wanted to help her, if she would just let him. He checked his bare wrist. There was no clock in the room, the whole trailer trapped in 1976.

When he checked the hallway again, both doors were closed; she was in one of the rooms, but he could not tell which one. This was too strange. It had to be late. He would leave; that's what he would do, what she wanted. Standing, he found his leg muscles tight. He stretched his arms over his head, twisted his neck, and then heard the door open.

Natalie stood in the hallway, the fluorescent lights on

her. Her skin shone, as if she were dusted with something, lightly oiled. Her thighs, her stomach, the straight line of her clavicle—he could see all of her skin. She wore only a short, white denim jacket; that was it, except for the tall snakeskin boots. Her hair was now shocking blond, almost platinum, parted straight in the middle, feathered back. One necklace, a single gold strand. She stood there, taller than him, and then stepped toward him, thinner than he would have thought. He tried to look away.

"This is too strange," he said.

"That doesn't mean anything."

"Natalie."

"Call me Patricia," she said. "Patricia McClain. As a triple Taurus, I'm very rebellious."

Up close, he saw that her eyelashes were false, impossibly long. She blinked rapidly, but she did not smile. Had her fingernails been so curved, so red, ten minutes before? She leaned against him and he felt the heat of her body, her whole length pressed against him, against his slacks, his polo shirt. He was sweating, her perfume thick around him.

"It's not like that," she said. "Not like anything you think. It's what you want, not me. It's all right, you can touch me. There. I'm not asking you to sleep over, only to come into the bedroom with me." She took his hand. "Come on. Everything's been prepared."

9.

CHRIS LAY FLAT ON HIS STOMACH, underneath the trailer. He felt Kayla's leg, pressing against his; she climbed over his back, brushing against him, the pressure of her body, and then lay down next to him. Leon was on her other side. The three stretched out, silent, the floor of the trailer close to their faces. They listened to the footsteps, the muted voices, then the grunting and gasping.

It was darker here, in the close space, than the darkness outside, the moonlight. Here, pieces of rotting garden hose, gravel, old tires and pieces of metal collected into the sharp dusty smell of things coming apart, breaking down. Chris tried to swallow, to clear his throat. It wouldn't clear. He shifted, following Kayla, to stay more directly underneath the noise overhead. A knocking began, like furniture legs jumping on the floor, a bed frame squeaking. Then there was Natalie's voice:

"I'll do what you want! This way? Should I bend my

knees, more?"

The three checked each other's reactions, in the dim light; they screwed up their faces in exasperation and disgust.

"Say it!" Natalie said. "Say it. Call my name."

"Patricia," the man said, then louder, "Oh, Patricia!"

Was there a third person in the trailer? Chris listened; he knew that was Natalie's voice, whatever she was saying. The floor above his face was flexing, bending down in rhythm, as if it might not hold. Chris felt Kayla's hand grasp his own, squeeze it, then let loose again.

"Wait!" Natalie's voice shouted, and then a door slammed.

The three tried to follow the footsteps; they rolled over and crawled on their stomachs, to the edge of the trailer. Suddenly, five feet from where they lay, the man emerged—wearing only white socks and briefs, he stumbled toward his car, his clothes and shoes in his hands. He looked back, once, with an expression of perplexity or shame, as if escaping.

"Let's go," Kayla whispered.

They pivoted and slid all the way across the trailer's width, to the back, and rolled out, bent over, dirt clapping from their clothes as they tried to cough without making noise. Leon was out front, then Kayla, Chris bringing up the rear. He saw Kayla stoop down, pocketing scraps of the magazines that littered the yard, and he caught up to her and Leon behind the abandoned house where they regained their skateboards and backpacks, their instruments in their cases. They did not speak. They kept going, running with the slick whisper of their nylon packs, the rattle and heavy thump of the pens and pencils and books.

They didn't slow until they were out on the road, beyond where they could even see the lights of Natalie's trailer. Still they moved in silence, all thinking about what they'd just heard and seen. Chris looked at Kayla's face; he wanted to reach out and take hold of her hand, at least to touch the skin of her arm. Things did not feel right since that day in Forest Park; balances were off. He felt that they had had sex, even if they hadn't. They could have, and now he couldn't tell if how he felt was Leon still acting weird or if it was what he, Chris, and Kayla had done together, or almost done. Should they tell Leon? Was it right for him not to know? Perhaps Leon should do it—or almost do it—once, to even it out, but then he'd have to do it with someone and probably that would have to be Kayla or Chris. And then that person would have done, or almost done it, twice. The balance would still be off.

"Why did he have to show up?" Leon said.

"We knew he would," Kayla said. "That's why we were there, remember?"

"Not tonight, I mean. In general."

Kayla shrugged; she shifted her flute case to her left hand, her skateboard to her right. "We were only two feet away from where they were doing it," she said.

"But really," Leon said, "so what? That's their problem."

"Are you defending her?" she said.

"That guy," he said, "Steven. He's the problem—he wants to make her like everyone else. You heard what he was saying before. She was playing with him, that's all. That doesn't really count."

"We can hope," she said, "but Natalie was still doing it. We can still be wrong about her, you know. I mean, I hope she didn't mean it, too, but I don't know. If we really expect her to show us some new ways to be, if she's some kind of example, that doesn't mean we have to accept everything she does. That would be pathetic. Mindless."

The three kept walking. Lights shone in the windows of the houses they passed, televisions flickering, dogs barking behind fences. The moon, not quite full, slid down through the tall trees.

"For instance," Leon said. "How she was using another name—that was her controlling it, playing with him. Or maybe that's her real name, maybe Natalie is just one she gave us."

The road beneath their feet turned to blacktop, and they set down their boards, the clocking of their tails and then the dull ricochet of the wheels, dropping, and then the three were pushing off, rolling past parked cars, under the tree branches and the dim stars.

They timed their trip to the bus stop perfectly, rode in silence for ten minutes, then were out again. Skating the long hill toward Leon's house, they carved long S-turns, crossing each other's lines. They cut in and out of the yellow circles the streetlights cast down. At the corner, they slowed, picked up their boards.

"Are we still studying biology tonight?" Chris said. "We still could, for a while."

"Cell division," Kayla said.

"I'm tired," Leon said. "Too tired."

"Tired?" Kayla said.

"And my parents are being weird, too." Leon scratched at the bristles of his head; the streetlight above made his round face shine, turned his eye sockets into dark smudges.

"Weird how?" Kayla said.

"They say I'm sneaking out at night, when I'm not. They say my clothes smell funny; they want to get me tested."

"For drugs?"

"For everything," he said. "Forget it."

"Parents," Chris said. "They don't know anything."

Leon shuffled off, not looking back. Kayla and Chris glanced at each other, watching him go, not calling to him.

"You want to go somewhere and study?" Chris said.

"Did you hear him?" Kayla said. "Are you seeing him like I'm seeing him?"

"It's because of us," Chris said. "He knows we're keeping a secret from him."

"Us?" she said. "No. We're not Leon's problem."

"So what is?"

"We'll find out," she said.

"I hope it's not too long."

"We're the answer," she said. "We're not the problem."

"You still want to study?"

"No," Kayla said, zipping her pack. "I think I'll head home, too."

She dropped her board, pushed off, and slid away, in and out of the streetlights, toward the bottom of the hill. Chris could hear her wheels after he could no longer see her, and after a moment the sound was gone, too.

10.

Natalie stood in her kitchen, one finger against the exposed wire of the outlet. It shocked a spark hot and sharp inside her arm, up past her elbow, through her rib cage, straight to her heart. And yet, despite the pleasure, the fuse had blown again; she headed toward the bedroom, the fuse box, to replace it.

Next to the bed, the unzipped boots lay like sections of snake, cut open. The silk sheets were on the floor, the tall wicker chair tipped over on its side. What had happened here? What was his name? Steven. When had it happened? This was evening—she could feel that in the air, the faltering light of dusk through the windows—but *which* evening? Turning, she picked up the phone. She dialed the number written on the wall to call for the time, and waited for the woman's voice. And the voice told her that two days had passed. Where had the time gone? She had lost it, not that it mattered; perhaps she had been sleeping. Forward, she was moving forward.

Patricia McClain's blond hair, her wig, lay forgotten on the bed. Natalie picked it up and carried it into the work-room, where she set it back on its styrofoam head. The chair, the boots—she set to retrieving and putting away the rest of Patricia's things. As she did so, she thought of Steven, the things he'd said. Had she quit her job so suddenly? Had she been somewhere she was not supposed to be?

Footsteps! Someone was coming; she could hear foot-steps outside, through the open window. It sounded like a three-legged person, or a person with a cane. Natalie went to the window. It was a boy, one of the boys, walking alone through the day's last light, aimed right at the trailer. He held a skateboard by its front wheels, its tail touching the ground with every other step. Spinning, Natalie grabbed Denise Michele's hair, the closest wig to the workroom's door—long and straight, slippery black. Asian hair.

Before he could knock, she jerked open the front door. That startled him—he took a step back, switched his skateboard to his other hand. Shorter than she was, barely, unsteady on the rickety porch, blinking his eyes, waiting for her to speak. His hair was shaved to black stubble, his body still holding on to its baby fat. He licked his lips. His eyes jerked around, his stubby fingers clenching and unclenching.

"Which one are you?" she said.

"Leon."

"Leon," she said. "You're alone."

"Yeah."

She looked past him, out into the darkness, not quite ready to take his word for it. "I didn't call Kayla," she said. "I don't have any work for you—there are specific times, you know. If you want money, I expect Kayla is giving you your share. That's how it has to work. Tonight I don't have anything."

"No," the boy said. "That's not why I'm here."

"And why are you here?"

"I don't know. I just wanted to come, so I did." Now he looked behind himself, as if she were looking at someone, as if he worried about being followed. "Was I wrong?" he said.

"I don't think so," Natalie said. "You better come inside; we'll try to figure it out."

She turned and he followed her, easy, as if this were familiar, as if they'd done it before. She could sense his body, sympathetic, behind her.

"I'd offer you something to eat or drink, but I don't have much right now. A glass of Tang?"

"Too grainy," he said. "Water, maybe."

He sat down in the only chair free of magazines, the chair where Steven had sat. He did not look down at the magazines; instead, he glanced carefully around the room, down the hallway and out the windows, as if memorizing it. When she handed him the glass of water, she stayed stretching across the table. She flipped open a couple of the issues in front of him, straight to the centerfolds. He sipped at the water, watching her. She unfolded the extra panel, and there her girls were, happy to be let loose. Daina, Karen, Hope, all their skin.

"Is this why you're here?" she said. "How would you like to see me? What do you want me to do?"

"I just wanted to come here, so I did," Leon said.

"Who do you think is the prettiest?" She pointed to her girls.

"The prettiest?" he said.

"Just choose one," she said, "and I'll be her for you. Just like her."

Leon swallowed, set the glass down on the March issue. "Don't you have a boyfriend?" he said.

"Not that I know of," Natalie said. She saw how he wasn't nervous, apprehensive; he was hardly looking at the girls. He seemed to be patiently waiting, almost humoring her.

"Can't you tell?" he said.

"You want something else."

"I don't know exactly what it is," he said.

"But you think I do."

Leon shrugged, his eyes darting toward the ceiling.

"We'll have to drive to get there," she said. "Maybe. If you think so."

"Yes," he said.

Then they were in the truck, the engine chortling, smoothing itself, the trailer sliding away behind them. Leon sat next to her, checking over his shoulder.

"No one's following," she said.

"I know. I've just never ridden in front. There's no one in back."

"Of course not."

She turned left on Johnson Creek just as the #75 bus came the other way, its windows alight, no one but the driver visible inside.

"I always wish it was seventy-six," Natalie said.

"Why?"

"Bicentennial," she said. "What year were you born, anyway?"

"Nineteen eighty-five."

Natalie drove, easing down the on-ramp to McLoughlin. "When I was a girl," she said, "we had the Bicentennial. That was different—everyone was really excited about the freedom it meant. It was wonderful, hopeful."

"That was really a long time ago," he said. "Wasn't that disco and everything?"

Static played low on the radio; neither of them moved to change it.

"The map!" she said.

"What?"

"In the glove compartment," she said. "There, unfold it."

She switched on the overhead light, squinted sideways—it was a street map of the city, an X marking where she lived, another over the place where they were going.

"Good," she said. "Thank you. Now put that away."

"You're welcome," Leon said.

"Where are your friends, do you think?" she said.

Leon rode calmly, staring straight ahead, his hands in his lap. It was as if he hadn't heard her question. They rattled north on MLK, past the Mexican restaurant on the right, La Carreta, past all the billboards of boring, hard-bodied girls in bikinis.

"You're wearing a wig," Leon said. "I know that."

"They're natural-hair wigs," she said. "All of mine are."

"From people's heads?"

"They're very expensive," she said. "Don't look surprised—just because I live in a trailer doesn't mean I have no money."

"That's not what I was saying."

Still south of Burnside, she hung a left, veering away from all the traffic, into dark, abandoned streets. High, high above she could already see the Towne Storage sign, the lion looking down. This was a risk; she had a feeling it was right, but she had been warned not to come here like this. Now that they were close, she remembered the warning.

"Are we going to the skatepark?" he said.

They were jostled together, the truck lurching through the cobblestones. She drove around parked trailers; the fruit wholesalers had all gone home. She dimmed her headlights, then parked a few blocks away, being careful. They left the truck next to a dumpster, under a door suspended in the air above. 'Well-hung Doors,' the lighted sign said. She had no time for that.

"Leon, where are you?"

"Here."

"Stay close. Take my hand."

She liked the feeling of him, anticipation coursing through his fingertips.

"What are we doing?" he said. "I won't do just anything, because you say."

"I know that," she said. "Trust me." Now she was pulling on his arm, making him keep her pace. She was stronger; he had to know that. "I'm impatient already," she said.

They'd reached the loading dock. She climbed up, lent him a hand. She stood at the door, keys trembling in her fingers as she tried to find the right one.

"Where is this?" he said, whispering.

"There's times I'm supposed to be here," she said. "This isn't one of them."

And then the door was open, shut behind them, and they were in the dark hallway, the fire safety lights spaced every thirty feet, dim, the only illumination, and she was counting down the numbers and he followed, since he didn't know which number it was. For a moment she thought of all the rooms they had passed, and all the cubicles above and below them—people's things, dead parents' furniture, photographs, secrets—and then she looked up and the number stared right at her, right there on the door. The key! Her fingers would not be still; she made them work. She turned the key. She pushed the door open and the air smelled of metal, ferrous splinters, sharpened dirt.

"Ready?" she said.

"Yes."

She hit the lights and the small room was there, instantly in front of them.

"It's the wire," Leon said.

She had seen the room when it held more. The wire was still wound in balls, like giant skeins of shining, bristly yarn. It was divided into two piles, right and left. The pile on the left was much smaller. Loose strands covered the floor, like in a barbershop where hair was metal. Natalie closed the door. She breathed in the thick smell of the copper, raspy in her throat. She did not want to take the time to teach him—could it be taught?—or to explain; she wanted to cross the room and take hold of it, to press it to her skin.

"Touch it," she said, nudging him to step closer.

He went to the larger pile first. He put his hand on a ball of wire, shifting it on the floor. He looked up at her.

"Is this all the wire we collected? Is this all ours?"

"Maybe," she said. "Some of it, anyway. Try the other."

Leon stepped sideways. He seemed tired, bored and impatient, ready for something to happen. Bending down, he placed his hand on a skein of wire in the smaller pile. He smiled and closed his eyes. He placed his other hand on the wire. His eyes opened, tears thick in them.

"This is different," he said.

"I knew you'd know it." Natalie hit the light switch and immediately dropped to the floor. On all fours she crossed the space, collided with Leon, went over the top of him, took hold of the wire.

"The lights," he said. "What? Hey!"

"I don't want to draw attention," she said. "There's probably a night watchman somewhere. Besides, your eyes won't help you here."

They settled. She could feel him, close in the darkness, but they were not touching. She could hear his breathing, and she could hear her own. The air around them hissed and sparked. Time passed; did it pass?

She did not hear the footsteps. She did not hear the key in the door, not even the hinges as they swung open. Suddenly the light spilled in, the frame of the door and the silhouette inside it—a person, a man, his long arm slapping the wall, searching for the light switch.

For a moment, none of them could see, startled by the brightness. Natalie realized that her shirt was unbuttoned, her bare stomach pressed to the ball of wire. Her wig was next to her on the floor; she put it back on, and buttoned herself, and realized that Leon was stretched out flat—one ball of wire behind his neck, one under his back, one beneath his legs. He wore one shoe; his T-shirt was tangled around his neck.

"Holy crow," she said.

"Whoa, whoa—wait!" The man at the door took a step back, retreating into the hallway.

Now she was able to see him: he was very tall, gaunt, his hair slicked back, his head almost reaching the top of the door frame. He wore dark, creased slacks, a white dress shirt, his mouth set in a straight, serious line. He pulled something, a piece of paper, from his pocket and squinted, reading it. His black beard was precise, pointing down at the floor where his narrow black shoes were just as sharp, pointing at her like two daggers. He stepped forward again, into the room, looking them over.

"No one's supposed to be here," he said. "That is very clear in the document."

She certainly had not seen him before, and yet he seemed familiar. His voice was a shifting tenor, and clipped, slightly Spanish, the words strange and second-hand. He set his eyes on her.

"Listen," she said, "I know what we agreed, on the phone. I realize I've overstepped, here."

"You and I," he said. "The two of us have not communicated by telephone."

"You're not the one who calls?" she said, but already she knew that this voice was different, that this man was not acting or putting her on. He seemed too odd, somehow, to suspect of duplicity.

"I am Victor," he said. "Victor Machado. I just work for him."

"For whom?" she said. "I'm Natalie."

"Well," the man said, "I don't know his name, of course."

"What does he look like?"

Victor looked away; he squinted again at the piece of paper in his hand.

"I'm Leon," Leon said. He was sitting, now, trying to

tie his shoe.

"What's he doing with the wire?" Natalie said. "And is that pile there just scrap?"

"Maybe," Victor said. "I do not do that part, I don't think. No." He stepped closer to her, then paused halfway. His hand came up, as if everything should pause, as if it were impossible for them to go anywhere. Turning, he disappeared into the hallway and returned pushing a large, yellow wheelbarrow made of metal.

"Enough questions!" he said. "Whatever you were doing, it is now time to cease, so that I am able to do this thing that I've been told to do." He set the wheelbarrow down, between her and Leon. "It is the wire on the left," he said, "that I'm to take. This I have been told. Excuse me."

"We're not hurting anything," Natalie said.

"We're the ones who brought it here," Leon said.

Victor ignored them. As he touched the first ball of wire, however, Natalie saw his eyes flicker, his lips tighten and curl—and she knew that he knew, also, that he was the same, or shared some kind of similarity. He saw her watching his expression and turned his face away. He did not slow. He piled the balls of wire in a pyramid, fitting them all in the wheelbarrow; slowly, he pivoted the heavy load on the black rubber wheel and began pushing it from the room.

Natalie was on her feet, Leon next to her. They followed Victor and the wire out through the door and down the hallway, onto the loading dock.

"Please," Natalie said. "Don't say that I—that we were here. We didn't change anything."

Victor backed up a white Chrysler K-car to the loading dock. A sticker marked its bumper: RENT-A-WRECK. He began to load the wire into the open trunk, the suspension sagging under the weight. The trunk was too full to close, so he wired it down. Last, he wedged the wheelbarrow into the back seat, kicking it with his pointed shoes, forcing it to fit.

"There's no reason to say anything," Natalie said. "No reason to tell."

Victor looked up to the loading dock where she stood with Leon, his expression incredulous. "You think I could?" he said. "That I could just tell him? I am a listener—I listen. He tells me things. It is not my place to tell him. That is a preposterous notion."

Victor climbed into the car, started the engine, and slowly pulled away. Natalie and Leon stood watching him go; the car's red taillights winked once, at the intersection, and then it turned a corner, out of sight. A few stars shone down, the moon lost in clouds, the night going cool. Reaching out, Natalie touched Leon at the back of his cool, sweaty neck, and pulled him closer. She straightened a thin strand of wire, a piece that she'd worked loose; she twisted the ends together, a necklace for him.

"Don't worry," she said, whispering still. "There will be more."

11.

"BLINDFOLDING YOU," Heather said. "That would be interesting, something to try."

She was sitting across from Steven, sorting through papers on her desk, reading them with her fingers. The Portland offices of The Seeing Eye were made up of three desks in this one windowless room. Carefully arranged papers covered the desks and tables, but the only writing on them was Steven's. Mostly the writing was Braille, the raised nubs hinting at messages he could not understand, sentiments mysterious and tantalizing.

"Sounds promising," he said.

"Or maybe the blindfold wouldn't be such a great idea," she said. "Since you might really want to watch me, to see me not seeing you."

The first time, the only time they'd been together, outside of work—on the houseboat—Heather had hesitated to even kiss him good night. Here at the office, with the constant possibility of interruption, people coming and going, she was freer with her flirtation and innuendoes.

"You never told me how your date went," she said.

"What?" he said.

"With your friend from San Jose."

"Natalie?" he said. "I wouldn't call it a date. It was all right. I doubt I'll see her again, though."

"Why not?"

"Are you trying to provoke me?" he said.

"Maybe. I'd just like to know why you wouldn't see her again."

"I'd rather spend more time with *you*."

"First," Heather said, "tell me what happened."

Steven sighed, exasperated. "She wasn't really how I remembered her," he said, "and she didn't really want to be reminded of her life before, or anything about that, so I think seeing me made her uncomfortable."

Heather pulled her thick, dark hair into a loose pony-tail, then stood and crossed the room; her body had its own memory—she swiveled her hips sideways in her yellow skirt, turning the corner of her desk. She brushed against Steven, reached out to touch his arm, gauging the distance, but did not sustain the contact.

"So I'm your only girl now?" she said.

"Exactly," he said, trying to get her to be serious. "When are we getting together again?"

"I need to practice with Ross," she said.

At the sound of his name, the dog stood up from

where he'd been sleeping, beneath the table. He panted, his thick pink tongue hanging out. His tail slapped the wall with a dull sound that was the perfect equivalent of his expression. Heather clipped the leash to his collar and the two of them went through the door, leaving Steven behind. He looked at the white walls, bare except for one plaque—THE DOG DOESN'T BELONG TO YOU, YOU BELONG TO THE DOG—and a piece of paper he'd taped up, a quotation from Helen Keller: "I have touched several lions in the flesh, and felt them roar royally, like a cataract over rocks."

Alone, he sifted through the papers on his desk, but had a hard time concentrating on the fund-raising mailing he was doing; his thoughts turned from Heather to Natalie, back and forth. More than a week had passed since he'd visited Natalie in the trailer. It had taken him by surprise; how could it not have? Her circumstances alone – the trailer, the rusted pickup truck—had destabilized him, and then there were the wigs, and the name she wanted to be called, all her poses and demands.

Standing, he walked around the room, swinging his arms, trying to shift his thoughts through physical movement. He went on, through the door, into the hallway. Out back, there were two chain-link kennels, empty now. Mostly the work here concerned coordinating the people who raised the puppies for the first eighteen months, before their formal training began. Also, The Seeing Eye helped the blind who already had dogs in the city. Steven answered questions on the phone, and helped write grants, and paid bills.

He hit the elevator button, then decided not to wait and climbed the stairs, two at a time. On the second floor, he walked down the hallway, past the dentist's office. He stopped at the far end of the hall, where a window over-looked the street.

Heather was below, crossing toward him, being led by Ross. The two of them were jaywalking, practicing "intel-ligent disobedience," where the dog was instructed to go forward, yet disobeyed the command because he sensed danger. It was the hardest thing to learn—to disobey one's master, for the master's own good—but Ross was getting the hang of it. Heather was still alive, after all, now step-ping onto the curb in her black sandals, eyes hidden behind her dark glasses. She spun Ross around, to cross again; the dog's red vest clashed with her yellow skirt.

Cars sped by, their colors blurring. A bus lumbered past, an advertisement for the zoo on its side. Ross stood still, not letting Heather cross. A pedestrian, a young man, paused on the sidewalk behind her, concerned; rather than asking if she needed help, though, he walked away, after a moment, careful not to appear condescending. Steven knew that feeling.

Leaning in, he touched the glass with his fingertips; the blind could tell windows from mirrors by vibration. Could he? He opened his eyes: the street cleared, and Ross took Heather across again. At the far side, they spun around. Heather's face was upturned, bright in the sun, and she was smiling slightly, as if she were aware that Steven was watching her.

12.

KAYLA PULLED OUT A SCRAP of magazine from where it was tangled, deep under the vines. Her expression turned from hopeful to dismissive.

"Just an advertisement," she said. "Fred Meyer." Balling up the paper, she threw it deeper into the blackberry bushes.

It was Saturday, hot, the middle of the afternoon. Chris and Kayla sat together, hidden in the vines; they'd already eaten all the berries—gritty, not quite ripe—within reach, and they were sitting on their skateboards, shields against the thorns. Fifty yards from the river, they faced the houseboats docked there. Waiting. Chris watched Kayla as she stuck her fingertip with a thorn. Dark red blood welled up, and she smeared it away against the skin of her leg. They both wore cutoff shorts; her calves were smooth, shaven, while dark hairs grew on his. He picked up the binoculars and checked the boat in the harbor.

"What if he's not even in there?" he said.

"Let's wait a little longer."

"Should we try to talk to him, if he comes out?"

"I don't know that, yet," Kayla said. "We probably shouldn't even let him see us, or notice us, for now. "Sorekara kare wo koroshu." She laughed.

"No te puedo entender cuando hablas japonés," he said.

Kayla took out her notebook and began writing in it. She looked out toward the river, then wrote some more. Chris could not tell if she was wearing makeup, thin black lines around her eyes; it looked like it, but he decided not to ask. He scratched his head—his hair was growing back now, and that made him think of Leon. Leon had not shown at the meeting place, and they had not waited for him. The three had strict rules about being on time.

He checked through the binoculars again. The Water-lelie was made of dark wood; brass circled the windows, all the fittings. A canoe was lashed to one side, a barbecue grill on deck. As Chris watched, a door opened in the cabin, and Steven stepped out, wearing jeans but no shirt. He stretched his arms out in front of him, as if he'd awakened from a nap.

"There he is," Chris said.

"Is he looking at us?"

"No; he's just looking up the dock, like someone might be coming."

"No one's coming, though."

Steven walked back and forth on the deck, checking

the ropes and knots, staring down into the dark water of the harbor.

"What'd he just pick up?" Kayla said. "What's he holding? A rabbit?"

"A cat, I think."

"A cat! That's just like him. Let me see." Kayla took the binoculars and leaned forward a little, to get that much closer. "He's so repugnant," she said. "He's everything that's wrong. I can't see how Natalie can even stand to talk to him, let alone—" She shivered rather than completing the sentence.

Below, Steven went back into the cabin, and they could no longer see him. Out on the river, beyond the houseboats, a scull jerked past, eight girls from Lewis and Clark or Portland State rowing in unison as a girl in back shouted through a bullhorn.

"Hot," Kayla said, setting the binoculars down, shading her eyes with her other hand.

"Why are we even watching him?" Chris said. "Because of Natalie?"

"No," Kayla said. "Natalie—she's good for money, as long as it lasts, but we've seen how she is. She's not going to teach us anything new; she's turning out to be just another adult."

"So, why?"

"Leon," she said. "Because you saw how Leon is about Natalie, and Natalie's into this sailor, and so you know we just have to find out what we can, follow it through."

Chris reached out and touched Kayla's leg. He ran his hand down its smoothness and clasped her ankle.

"That's my ankle," Kayla said.

"I know," he said, letting go.

"Let's not get started again." She turned her head to look at him, her expression calm and tired.

"Right," Chris said. His back ached; he wanted to lean over, but there were thorns in every direction. Instead, he unzipped his pack and took out the book, the paperback that Kayla had lent him.

"I read it," he said.

"And?"

"I don't know," he said. "I'm not sure what happened."

The cover showed a painting of blue water, and waves, and boats in a harbor, bare masts sticking into the sky; it was different, but also close to the scene they were watching. Above the painting was the title, *The Sailor Who Fell from Grace with the Sea*, and the author's name, Yukio Mishima. At the top of the cover, it read, "A Novel of the Homicidal Hysteria that Lies Latent in the Japanese Character." Kayla reached out to point at these words.

"Kind of misleading," she said. "That's how they sell books, I guess. Watashi tachi wa amerika-jin. Watashi tachi no kokoro ni naniga aru no kashira."

Chris turned the book over; on the back, a yellow banner read "Now a Major Motion Picture! Starring Sarah Miles and Kris Kristofferson!"

"I wish you wouldn't speak Japanese," he said.

"Then learn it; we could speak it together."

"I thought we decided I should learn Spanish. I should master the one before starting another."

"Fine," she said. "And I know what you mean about the book—you never find out what happened to the kids. Were they right to follow their beliefs? Were they wrong? Did they get in trouble, or did something else happen? How did they feel?"

"The ending is kind of fast," Chris said.

Kayla reached out and took the book from him. "Did you see this page here, where I bent the corner back?"

"Yeah," he said, "only I couldn't tell what you thought was important."

Kayla read it aloud: "There was a label called 'impossibility' pasted all over the world, and they were the only ones who could tear it off, once and for all."

"Right," Chris said.

"Doesn't that sound familiar?" she said. "I'm going to write it down."

Kayla began writing in her notebook again. Chris leaned forward to retie his shoelace; when he tugged at it, it broke, and he had to tie another knot, to fit the tattered end through an eyelet.

"One more week of school," he said. "You think we'll ever get to that Bartók? Those folk songs? Finally a piece with decent solos for clarinet and flute, and I bet we never even get to play it."

"There's our sailor again," Kayla said. "There he is."

Steven was back on the boat's deck, holding a phone to his face, talking.

"I don't have the headset," Kayla said, still squinting through the binoculars. "But even if I did, it's too light out; we'd get caught. Can't even see the line, anyway. Oh—it's a cell phone. I wonder what he's saying. Look at him!"

Even with his bare eyes, Chris could tell that Steven was angry. He gestured with his free hand and paced back and forth, turning quickly. He'd put on a yellow t-shirt, a baseball cap against the sun; he tore the cap from his head, waved it in the air, then jerked it down tight again.

"I bet he's talking to Natalie," Kayla said.

"I wonder if he called her or she called him."

"The way he left that night," she said, "I don't know. Oh—look, look!"

Steven dropped the phone to his side, his face turned toward the dock.

"He's smiling," Kayla said. "Just like that. Look at her."

A tall woman was walking out the dock, hesitantly, toward Steven. She wore sunglasses, a white sleeveless dress; dark curls fell over her shoulders.

"That's not Natalie," Chris said. "Is it?"

"She's blind," Kayla said.

She handed the binoculars to Chris, and then he could see the long white cane the woman held, the way she switched it back and forth, over the water. Steven stepped up onto the dock to greet her. He held out his arms and kissed her cheek.

"What's he doing with someone else?" Chris said.

"Does it matter?" Kayla said.

"I guess not," Chris said. Through the binoculars, he watched Steven lead the blind woman onto the boat. The two of them disappeared into the cabin.

13.

CHRIS SAT IN THE BACK of the truck with Leon, looking forward into the cab. Natalie stared through the windshield, her arms straight, driving. Tonight her hair was honey blond, the sides feathered back. Kayla had her head stuck out the passenger window, so her long hair stretched out, solid, parallel to the highway slipping below. They were heading north, past the airport, into the darkness—headlights came and went as the city fell away behind them.

Leon's trombone case rested open, the hinges straining. He pulled out the orange headset, tossed Kayla's Japanese novel to one side. He tore a length from a roll of duct tape and began attaching a flashlight to the top of a baseball cap.

"You read it?" Chris said, pointing to the book.

"Kind of."

"It's pretty much exactly what we've been saying, about adults and everything."

"I just don't feel like reading, much," Leon said. "Lately, I can hardly even listen to music—it all sounds kind of too fancy to me."

"So you're not practicing?"

"Summer's here," Leon said. "School's out."

They turned off the highway near a sign that promised waterfalls; a couple miles farther, they pulled over. Natalie opened the back and Leon and Chris climbed out, stretching.

It was silent for a moment, everyone taking in the surroundings. Far away down below, the Columbia's dark waters—wider and wilder than the Willamette's—were torn by wind and climbing over themselves, eager to reach the ocean. The highway was distant now, below on the near bank, headlights snaking along. Thick electrical wires filled the air, stretching all the way across the gorge, the river, all the way to Washington and back again; the wires ran up from dams, from tower to tower.

Closer to where the four of them stood, an electrical substation lay surrounded by chainlink fence, partially hidden. It hummed, its white porcelain insulators in the air, its thick transformers shadowy on the ground.

"Seems like no one's around," Natalie said, "but there's more risk, here, than it looks. I'll be back in less than an hour. You can handle it, Leon."

With that, she climbed into the idling truck, shifted into gear, and was gone.

"What's with her all of a sudden using your name?"

Kayla said to Leon. "Usually she only knows my name."

Chris looked from Kayla to Leon, and back again. He knew that Natalie had had to go searching—early in the morning, down to the skatepark under the bridge—in order to find Kayla, who was supposed to call every day. There hadn't been any work for a while, now, so she hadn't called for over a week. Having Natalie unhappy with her made Kayla edgy, too.

"Look at your head," she said, still talking to Leon. "Did you get another haircut?"

"No," Leon said.

"We should start," Chris said.

"Look at Chris," Kayla said, "his hair is already all growing back, and you're still bald."

"Grows slow," Leon said. "So what?" He put on his cap, flicked the flashlight. He looked over at Chris and the beam of light was blinding. It was impossible to look back at him, to see his face.

"It doesn't matter," Chris said. "She probably knows all our names—it's like the tenth time we've done this, after all."

"What are you doing?" Leon said.

Kayla was putting on the climbing spikes; she'd grabbed them while Leon fooled with his flashlight.

"You're getting too reckless," she said. "Besides, we should split up the climbing."

"What about Chris?"

"I already have one spike on," she said.

Chris looked away, up into the sky. The stars were brighter, sharper, away from the lights of the city.

"You think there'll be any lightning?" he said.

"There's no lightning," Leon said. "Come on—it doesn't even smell like rain." He pointed down the slope, toward the substation. "Let's do the tower, there, on the other side. That'll be easier to climb."

"It'll also be about a hundred times more dangerous," Kayla said. "The voltage is stepped down on this side. Help me here, Chris."

"Dangerous?" Leon said. "We've done this so many times, just like Chris was saying."

Chris helped Kayla with the belt. Walking in the long spikes, she leaned on him. He boosted her onto the pole, and she climbed slowly at first, getting her balance straight, remembering.

When she had gotten halfway to the top, Chris stepped back. It was dark all around him, no movements on the road or down near the substation. Past the substation, though, he saw a spot of light, slowly rising. It was Leon, on the tower, climbing, the hunched shape of his body clearing the treetops, barely darker than the night sky.

"Where's Leon?" Kayla called down.

"I can't see him," Chris said. "He's probably off somewhere, taking a leak. Don't look down."

Chris watched them both; he could think of nothing to do or say that would persuade anyone or change anything. Now Kayla had reached the top of the pole and had her clippers on the wire, straining to cut it. A hundred feet away, Leon stood even higher, just a silhouette; both hands free, he wrapped his legs around a metal support, no harness at all.

Below, between them, a blue glow spilled out from the base of the transformers in the substation. There was a crack, a rising whoosh coming off the ground, the light sparking and collapsing into itself, forming a fireball that shot upward. White, it cast the sudden black shadows of the trees, of the towers and poles. The fireball ricocheted inside the fence, across every wire, gaining speed and brightness, spinning toward the top, escaping. Chris held his breath. The ball of light leapt the tower where Leon held on; it kept on down the line, toward the lights of the distant city. It sped away, the wires crackling in its wake, getting smaller as the distance increased, a sound like a rip in the sky.

In moments, Kayla and Leon were down on the ground—safe, untouched. They ran with Chris along the shoulder of the road, in the direction that Natalie had gone. Their six feet pounded a rhythm. Distant sirens wailed. Chris hoped that Natalie had heard, that she had not gone too far. He glanced sideways at Kayla's face, scared and serious, and then Leon's—Leon was smiling as he half-skipped along, almost laughing, as if something wonderful had just happened. Oblivious, he didn't seem to notice that Chris was watching him; eyes wide, he seemed to be looking at nothing at all.

-∿-

Someone in the bar where Natalie sat thought they heard a gunshot, but she knew better; she felt the electricity pass overhead, the heat in the fillings of her teeth. She'd put songs on the jukebox—"Barracuda," "Fly Like an Eagle," "Takin' It to the Streets"—as a way to keep track of time, mostly, so she wasn't sorry to miss listening to them. Setting her glass of wine on the bar, she stood and walked out to the parking lot, to her truck, just as the lights inside shut down. She'd reach the kids in less than ten minutes, and they'd see how far the blackout ran, this time.

-∿-

Behind Steven, Heather came out of the boat's cabin, onto the deck. She could not see a thing, and he tried to explain it to her, the way a wave of darkness fell across the city, the power grid going a piece at a time, the sky suddenly darker and the stars more piercing.

-∿-

The power lines under the street were spitting, crackling. Victor Machado pulled himself away from them, up through a manhole. He did not replace the cover, but ran along the dark street, long arms dangling, toward Chinatown. He hoped that the man in the shop would be able to reassure him, would know what all this meant.

–√√√–

Chesterton sorted copper bracelets, sitting in Shanghai Shanghai, his shop in Chinatown. When the lights went out, he laughed his deep, baritone laugh. Barefoot, he stood and stepped around a display of jade, another of lacquer boxes. He pushed open the door and the brass bell rang. Heading out into the darkening street, he looked all around with satisfaction. This was the kind of event that could reap many injuries, that might produce copious amounts of high quality wire.

TWO

14.

THE BOAT DRIFTED SO SLOWLY from the harbor, so early in the morning, that it hardly seemed to be moving. Yet suddenly it was loose, not connected to the land at all, the gap of water growing wider. Slowly the boat found the current, the river's lazy pull; frayed lines, roughly cut, trailed loosely behind, through the dark water.

The air was still, the wind nonexistent. A plastic bag jerked silently along, keeping pace; the sparest shiver ran along the water's skin, it gently slapped the bow as the boat slipped beneath the Sellwood Bridge, between the concrete stanchions. It did not strike them—but, as it passed, a back eddy spun the boat, bow to stern, so a person standing on the bank could have read the name painted there: WATERLELIE.

A person high above the river would see how slow the current ran, the boat hardly moving, aimless and drunken and with sad purpose as it slid past the darkened amusement park, the shadowy Tilt-A-Whirl and unsteady rollercoaster, the black ribbon of the go-cart track and the distended tracks of the miniature train that looped through and lost themselves in the trees where, sitting on a picnic table, the night watchman watched the night. He smoked a cigarette (its tip bright, giving him away as he inhaled), but he was not facing the river, he did not see the boat as it—so small, all the dark water around it, alone and lonely on the river—slipped by.

Down the right channel, next to Ross Island, past the gravel pits, through cattails, its bottom brushed the sandy, muddy bottom; the boat slowed, but did not stop. Forgotten re-bar hooked up through the black water, clipped the propeller's pin, loosened it on its spindle. Now the forgotten lights of the city loomed to the left, the Ross Island Bridge behind and the shadow of the Hawthorne Bridge ahead, above. It was too early for commuters—only a few cars on the bridges, and no one inside them alarmed, half-awake—and the sun not even up. A waning sickle moon slanted its cold light down. The sky was charcoal; it was the hour of silhouettes.

And on the boat itself, on its deck and in its cabin, there was no movement. The cold moon shone through portholes, casting pale circles on the wooden floor. All was still, unaware of being adrift. Only the cat stirred. She walked the rail (counterclockwise, as the boat slowly spun clockwise) and she mewed in complaint, aware that something was not right and that it was beyond her to change it. She circled, talking to herself, pausing only to lick anxiously at her thin shoulders, resuming her pacing.

North, always moving north, the boat came upon the Burnside Bridge. Burnside, bisecting the city north from south. The bridge sat old and heavy across the river, the water in its shadow black, its underside so far overhead and yet seemingly barnacled, familiar with water. To follow this underside east, to the bank, would take a person directly above the skatepark. It was almost empty at this hour.

Only Kayla was skating, practicing, headphones tightly over her ears. A kick-flip into a drop-in, a fakie ollie with a shaky landing—the concrete flashed by, a blur; teeth gritted, she refused to bail. She rode it out, up the far wall, gathering herself, rising again atop the near wall, against the chain-link fence. She caught her breath, her hair long and black and straight, hanging down, her hands on her knees, her fingernails painted dark red. She brushed back her hair, recognized the distant boat sliding beneath the bridge.

"Kanojo wa hen-na hito desu ne," said the voice in her ears. Kayla smiled, then spat, just missing a car parked below. Again, the kick-flip, the fakie ollie, her thoughts spinning quicker, her landing solid this time, straight to a tail slide across the lip.

She did not see the boat reach the Steel Bridge; it was around a bend, out of her sight, gradually picking up speed, angled toward the Columbia, and then perhaps the ocean. It had been lucky at the other bridges, but here the openings funneled the currents differently, in a tangled braid; the boat caught somehow, sideswiped a concrete piling. The sound was small; no one heard it. There was a jolt, a clutching, and then the boat listing to one side, still slipping north.

Almost another hour passed before it came to rest, alongside other boats, in a small harbor along the Sauvie Island channel. It nestled, rubbing alongside these other boats, whose residents were asleep. The cat paused, uncertain whether to attempt a leap to the dock. She resumed her circling of the cabin. The windows were open, and the curtains lifted and twisted upon themselves, stretching toward the brass bedstead that swayed slightly with the water's motion. It was bolted down, as were the bedside tables. The quilt had been kicked onto the floor, and under the sheets Steven began to stir. He rolled over and sat up; he'd dreamed there was a storm, or perhaps there had been a storm, the boat shifting in the harbor. Before he even put his feet down on the slanted floor he knew something was wrong.

He stepped onto the deck and saw how the lines had come undone, that the boat was loose. He looked at the other boats around him, then turned to look at the river. It took a moment to realize that this was not where he had gone to bed last night, that these were different boats in a completely different harbor.

The lines sank straight down in the water. He pulled one up, then another. They were shredded, roughly cut, all undone and worthless. He dropped them back in and they went under with pathetic splashes. Next, he walked around the cabin and looked at the dent on the port side, the bend in the bow's shape. He started the engine and shifted into reverse; the motor was fine, fired right up, but there was nothing—no movement, just the worthless whine of the spindle spinning like a naked stick under-water. The propeller was gone.

"Excuse me!" he shouted to a man down the dock. "Where am I? Can I get a hand, here?"

Once the boat was secured, he tried his cell phone, but the battery was dead. He collected change from the top of his dresser, from the galley counter, and set off down the dock, up a swaying ramp, toward a parking lot. The pay phone was next to a soda machine. First he called The Seeing Eye, and listened to Heather's voice on the machine, calmly offering information about dogs, possible questions and answers, hours of operation—the sun wasn't even up yet; it would be a while before they opened, and he could call Heather at home but he couldn't exactly ask her for help. What could she do for him? In any case, it helped to hear her voice.

Steven bought an orange soda, took a long, cold drink, and coughed. He spotted the bus stop—the bus that would take him downtown—and then looked down at the boat again, the river. There were explanations to be made, damage to be considered, a temporary slip to be found. He went back down the ramp, to the dock, double-checked the knots on the lines he'd borrowed. On board, he found a duffel bag, then began taking some clothes from the dresser, collecting the few valuables he possessed. He wasn't certain where he would stay, only that it wouldn't be here. He couldn't quite get his head around it—someone had cut him loose in the night, set him adrift. He didn't even know that many people in Portland; it was possible that whoever had done it had believed the boat's owner was inside, or at least had something to settle with that old Dutchman. It had to be some kind of mistake.

Steven was halfway down the dock when he heard a low cry behind him. The cat watching him from the rail, perched there with only her eyes moving, tail twitching. He switched the duffel bag to his left hand, then picked up the cat with his right. She pressed her warm body against him, purring, as he walked to the bus stop.

They waited half an hour or so, and the driver didn't even listen to Steven's explanation, didn't question him about the cat. Steven walked down the aisle of the empty bus and sat down in the back.

He tried to think ahead, to plan. The bus lurched along, parallel to the river, moving south. To the right, Forest Park rose thick and green; the St. John's Bridge stretched over the shadowy river on the left. The sun began to rise, sharp in his eyes.

They slid through the sleepy industrial area, the docks, and up through Chinatown. Steven rested, leaning his forehead against the window. It was at a traffic light that he saw her—the streets were almost empty, and her battered pickup idled next to the bus, waiting for the light to turn green. Natalie.

He had neither expected nor desired to see her again, and now she was only ten feet away, oblivious, slightly below him. Her window was open, her hair long and strawberry blond, full, her sheer blue blouse embroidered with daisies that hardly covered her breasts. Steven leaned forward to see her expression, and realized that she was not alone. In the passenger seat, the side of a man's face was barely visible; it was only a boy, actually—sitting there, his hands in his lap, looking bored—with a hint of baby fat in his smooth white face, his dark hair shaved to the barest stubble. And then the light changed, and Natalie's truck pulled away. He couldn't imagine what she was up to, this early in the morning, and he didn't really care to.

Reaching up, he pulled the cord, then thanked the driver and climbed down to the sidewalk. The cat awakened, but did not fight him. The streets were mostly empty, people just rousing themselves; a garbage truck rattled around a corner, hardly slowing. Steven could see the building that housed the office, half a block away, the sign with one big eye staring out, superimposed on the shape of a dog.

15.

A WEEK AFTER THE INCIDENT with the sailor's boat, Kayla skated alone under the Burnside Bridge. This was where she did her thinking, and she had plenty of thinking to do. Her long, black hair in four braids, snaking around her head, pink plastic barrettes aclatter, she flew across the park and to the top of the concrete wall, pulling a 50-50 grind into a ten-foot board slide—the gnarled scrape of her metal trucks on the concrete, then the hollow smoothness of the sliding wood, then rocking down and the roar of the wheels again.

Sometimes in the early mornings it sounded like ten people skating, but it was only Kayla, her wheels echoing with the roar of water. She gasped, and huffed, and softly sighed, yet she could not hear herself, she could not hear her wheels. Her headphones were tight in her ears, the Walkman on her belt playing Stravinsky's Fireworks, but she was not paying attention to that, either; the music spun loose, lost in some distant part of her brain. Kayla was thinking too hard to listen, her mind split between skating—the concrete, her body, the air—and making sense, the remembering and the looking ahead.

A semi-trailer full of fruit eased past, outside the fence; the driver slowed to watch, but Kayla did not notice. She popped out one end, up top, swerved around her backpack, her new platform-soled sandals—she skated in her Chuck Taylors, like always—and dropped back into a bowl. Her makeup was in the pack, and her other clothes, and her Japanese flashcards, her sunglasses, her cheap plastic bracelets and necklaces. Buried beneath it all was her notebook, full of facts and guesses about Natalie and, increasingly, notes about Leon, multiplying suspicions. The notebook showed how intertwined everything had become; on one of the last pages she'd taped in the newspaper article about the blackout they'd caused that night up by the Columbia. Thousands of people lost power; it took two days to get it straight again. And people were badly hurt: three phone linemen, working late, and nine others—a homeless kind of family living under a bridge in North Portland. Their illegal electrical lines, snaked out from a transformer box, hadn't been able to handle the surge. The wires had exploded like a bomb, the paper said, like a flood of electricity right over them, taking them all to the ground.

Some were still in the hospital—burned or recovering from heart attacks—and some might not make it out. As the days passed Kayla had not tried to find out more. She would not let herself; when she started to feel herself drifting in that direction, to sink, she choked it back. She would not let herself. No one knew why it happened, no one could trace the blackout's cause, and if those people were gone they weren't coming back. And she was here, kicking hard across the skatepark, rising up on the vertical section of the wall.

She tried a backside handplant, an invert, but she lost hold of her board and was caught there, upside down for a moment—the board flew end over end, landed on its wheels, rolled up the far bank as if ridden by a phantom—and she could smell the concrete, see the tiny forks and cracks like fissures in bone, and in that moment it seemed she might come down on her face, but momentum carried her legs up over her head, across in an arc, and she slid down on her knees, the toes of her shoes, all the way to the bottom. Her board zinged back to catch her in the ribs, perfectly timed.

Standing, she could feel her knees skinned, under her jeans, could feel the cool trickles of blood sliding down her shins. She tasted more blood, in the back of her throat; she spat, and the spit was clear; it just all made her think harder, and skate with more abandon, the pounding somehow bringing thoughts out of her. She climbed up, dropped in, kicked twice for speed. She shot up the wall and floated an ollie over the corner, swooping across, floating weightless in a long frontside carve across the wall, up where the Grim Reaper had been spraypainted over, where beneath the word FEAR there was only the black shape of a person, like a shadow with arms out wide. She sensed a movement behind her, and carved around, looked across to her things, where someone was now standing. Chris. He waved, watching her, his helmet loose in one hand, his skateboard in the other.

She swooped up, skidded next to him, slapped his shoulder.

"Been here long?" he said.

"I think I'm done."

"That ollie was big."

"Thanks," she said.

Flipping her board over onto its deck, she began to rummage through her pack. She took out a small folding mirror, opened it, and held it up. She moved it around in a slow circle, checking every angle, then took out a black pencil and traced her eyes. Next, she unsnapped her barrettes and let them fall, a handful of pink beetles clattering on the concrete. She began to brush out her hair, straightening her part.

"Those are your sandals?" Chris dropped his helmet so it bounced with a hollow sound, settling on the concrete next to the shoes. "I don't really know what you're getting at these days."

"We never agreed to all dress alike," she said, lipstick in hand. Her Hello Kitty T-shirt was tight across her chest. "Anata ni do are to wa itte nai wa," she said.

"Hey." Chris looked past her, pointing down to the street. "Is that Natalie down there?"

"No," Kayla said, at last looking away from the mirror. "That's not even a woman—just some homeless guy."

"Natalie," he said. "You never know what she'll look like."

"True," Kayla said.

"And it's been a while since we've seen her."

"I think we're done," she said.

"Done?"

"At least for a while. I think that's enough wire for a long time."

They'd worked for eight straight nights, collecting wire after the blackout, and then not for two weeks. Natalie had taken all the equipment back from them, even the phone headset.

"And it's good for us to get away from Natalie," Kayla said. "She's pathetic, when you really think about her."

"Right," Chris said.

"Maybe we could do the wire without her. Just collect it and turn it in."

"But we couldn't carry it," he said. "And we wouldn't know where to take it. We have to find something else."

"Something," Kayla said. "Something that'll help bring Leon back." She checked her face one more time. "Mashi. Kirei. Nan ni shite mo kawaii wa," she said, and then she folded the mirror and put it away. She unlaced her Chuck Taylors, stood, kicked them off, then unzipped her pants, pushed them down, and stepped out of them. She wore yellow panties. Dried lines of blood ran from her skinned knees, down her shins, marking her white ankle socks with red.

"You don't have to look away," she said.

"You can dye your hair black and paint your eyes slanted," Chris said, his voice quiet, "but you're not Japanese. And we hardly did anything to the sailor, nothing like the book. None of this is a real change."

Kayla reached into her pack and took out a short, plaid schoolgirl skirt. Red and green. She wrapped it around herself, hooked the belt. She didn't say anything for a moment, only looked away, across the gray concrete. The day was growing lighter, the shadows sharper, the cars louder on the bridge overhead. Then she bent down, buckling the thin straps of her sandals.

"So maybe the sailor has nothing to do with it." She stood, gaining four inches, and looked down at Chris. "We had to try something, at least—jinsei wa no kantan na singo to kesshin de naritatte iru. It's not like we can just do nothing."

"To do with *what*?" Chris said. "What are you talking about?"

"Leon," she said. "Everything."

"Leon? What do you mean? He didn't even help us with the sailor."

"What could he have done, really?" she said. "We were enough."

"That's not what I meant," Chris said. "What I meant was it used to always be the three of us."

"Right," Kayla said. "Is it him, or is it us? It's not like we can make him spend time with us."

"And it's not like he has new friends," Chris said. "Not that we know of."

"Do you think," she said, "do you think he might be seeing Natalie on his own?"

They had both noticed, during the last few jobs, how Natalie watched Leon, how familiar the two seemed.

"Working for her?"

"Or something."

"I guess so," Chris said. "It's possible."

"Even if he is," she said, "that's just a piece of it, whatever they're doing, whether we can, too. I don't care about her like I care about Leon."

"So," Chris said, "what are we supposed to do?"

"Help him, I guess. Try to understand what he's going through or something. I believe he's doing something."

"No," Chris said. "Come on, like drugs? Already his parents are on him, you know?"

"I mean really doing something," Kayla said. "It's not that we have to bring him back to be like us, necessarily; it might be that we have to go where he is, you know?"

"Like following him?"

"Kind of," she said. "That's part of it."

"Can't we just ask him?" Chris said.

"You know that doesn't work," Kayla said. "He's either

lying, or he's as clueless what his deal is as we are."

"Why would he lie?" Chris said.

"If it was me," she said, "I'd want the two of you to try, come after me."

"Me, too."

"What did he say?"

"When?"

"On the phone."

"Yesterday?" Chris said. "He didn't really say what he'd been doing. He was talking about maybe going to the planetarium today, or maybe Oaks Park."

"That rollercoaster's a joke," Kayla said. "You planning on getting some runs in before it gets crowded?"

Chris picked up his helmet and buckled it on, then set his board down gently. He dropped in and Kayla stood watching him go—his elbows bent sharp and rigid, his butt out, shakier than ever. He turned an awkward 180 on the far wall and came back, trying to decide what to do next, an expression of deep concentration on his face.

16.

CHESTERTON SAT IN HIS SHOP, Shanghai Shanghai, one lamp casting a narrow circle of light onto his notebook. His hands were huge, and he wore a gold watch on each wrist, along with several copper bracelets. He wrote with a quill pen, a blue feather—he enjoyed the pretension, the affectation of it—and sat on a stool, hunched over next to his cash register, the notebook open on the counter. As he wrote, he listened to the police scanner, the officers bantering and serious, calling out the codes he'd memorized; he kept his ears pricked for any mention of electrocution.

His words, he chose them carefully, laying them down for posterity, attempting to account for the slipperiness of the situation he described, to account for all that he did not know. How little he knew was apparent to him, and how quickly things could change. He moved slowly; he tried to never anticipate. These days, for instance, he'd realized that sometimes, when he talked, little bubbles of saliva floated from the tip of his tongue. This was new, as if the shape of his mouth were changing, the way he talked, or how he said the things he said, the force and feeling behind it all. Had his writing changed, at the same time? He could not tell, but he did find it a complicated pleasure, simultaneously satisfying and dissatisfying—this, he believed, was a relationship to aspire toward with regard to all things.

The metal grates outside were pulled down; he could not see out, no one could see in. The lamp reflected off the top of his dark, bald head. The shadowy, cluttered shelves around him held dusty acupuncture charts, plaster skulls, folding fans, Tiger Balm. Oils and tinctures and potions bearing mysterious names and promises—they were little more than water and artificial colors—and dried herbs that were years old, that were mostly ground to powder. Flip-flops, dented rice cookers, chipped teapots, dried fish with startled eyes, Chinese calendars far out of date.

He hated the New Age movement, but depended on the mystical-minded, those with a predisposition to believe. That was why he'd chosen Chinatown. Were his goods authentic? He didn't worry about that, or even if the operation made much money. He wanted to blend in, and he left most of the ordering to Henry Yee, the Chinese man he hired to front the store. Did Chesterton himself stand out, draw attention? Certainly—tall and broad and blacker than black, he did not easily fit. The store needed an Asian face, and that was Henry, who was also good-natured, and sharp, and enjoyed the irony of it all.

The only part of the shop that Chesterton cared about, the only section that Henry didn't handle, were the items made of copper. The bracelets, the anklets and arm cuffs. They were sold, ostensibly, to ease arthritis and other aches and pains, to enhance clear-headedness and focus, to reverse impotence and falling hair. The wider the bands, the more powerful and expensive. Chesterton made them himself, melted down the copper wires in a cauldron upstairs, over an amped-up hot plate; he stamped the inside with "Made in China" or with nonsense ideograms or misspelled, authentic-looking palliatives: SERINETY, INSITE, MEDETACION.

Now, writing, Chesterton paused. He thought he heard something, some motion beneath the floorboards, some hidden hinges. He paused, then continued with his argument; the three copper bracelets on his wrist rattled as he wrote.

The shelves holding the bracelets were carefully dusted. The bracelets ranged in price from five to forty dollars, all except the ones on the far end. These were less attractive, ugly on purpose—thinner, rougher, and yet attached to the shelf by steel cables, to prevent theft. Their price was five hundred dollars. People asked him why, but he did not tell them. Not even Henry Yee understood; he believed it was a joke, a marketing strategy he could not grasp.

There were people who did not need to ask why these

ugly bracelets were different, or cost so much, who could sense this by merely touching the copper. It was these people whom Chesterton sought out. It was of these people that he wrote.

For years he had studied them; only recently had he gained real insight, however, had he collected the beginnings of an adequate base of knowledge. His list was almost one hundred individuals long; he knew there were more, but did not allow himself to estimate.

He listened to the police scanner. Each day, he checked the newspaper for electrical accidents, and he kept track of every electrocution. Upstairs, overhead, there were two rooms. In the larger one, he conducted his experiments; the other was full of books on electricity, its use and misuse. Articles on electroshock therapy, the victims of lightning strikes, and the currents that occurred naturally within organisms. On the walls of this room were topographic maps of Portland and the surrounding area. These maps were covered in pins with different-colored heads. White for electrical incidents, blue for injuries, red for deaths. A cluster of red, for instance, marked the spot beneath the bridge in North Portland, the most recent tragedy. The blue pins, the "Affected," were the ones that intrigued Chesterton, that held out promise.

It was almost too much to synthesize, to boil down and filter, and yet he knew that he must not shy from the attempt. That was why he documented his findings and hypotheses, why he took the time to write, why he allowed his writing to spur new possibilities for exploration.

I. AN ATTEMPT AT AN INTRODUCTION

A hidden world exists all around us, people whose motivations, desires and understandings differ from our own—perhaps this notion seems self-evident, but I write not of the fact of this difference. I write of its extent and its degree.

I strive to humbly describe and delineate this difference, to speculate on how the lives of these people—hereafter identified as the Affected, for purposes of clarity—stretch beyond our own, and what we might learn from them.

I must stress that the Affected are not forthcoming about their condition, that one must take what one can from them. They are not a reflective people.

Allow me to lay out a tentative structure for these written investigations: I will begin with preliminary remarks, provide some individual examples, proceed to my own hypotheses and experiments and, from there, speculate about future implementations and the like. I cannot of course promise to cleave exactly to this plan. I must maintain flexibility, and follow each possibility as it demands attention or promises insight.

Some may question how my interest in this matter was spurred, or ignited, or even how someone who is UnAffected would ever gain insight into or achieve recognition of such an insular society. Is it enough to say that I've always had my suspicions? I am a man who has, in my past, personally experimented with electricity, who has worn magnets in my shoes, my underwear, placed them in my mattress. I have always felt the electricity within me, the currents that enable motion, that fire the synapses, leaping gaps in my mind— and I believe there must be ways to amplify this energy, to improve me or perhaps change the tenor or kind of my experiences. So: I led myself to the Affected, in a way.

From this suspicion arose an awareness, and awareness was the first real, substantive step. Perhaps in another, later place I will document the gleanings, the gradual piecing together; here, I seek to move with more decisive rapidity.

Am I able to identify the Affected by sight? Their twitchiness, their indecisiveness? Sometimes, perhaps. Often the bracelets here in my store allow an easy differentiation—a browsing customer suddenly identified—and other times I have found them by other means, even by chance. Denise, Jonathon, Walter. Underground, or at remote substations, or near dams, late at night, lost in the hydroelectric hum. I think of my Victor Machado, who came to ask me for work when no one else would employ him—sometimes I wonder if the Affected are drawn to me! And Natalie, whom I first saw lurking around a power plant, whom I later witnessed tampering with neighborhood power distribution systems. I followed her for quite some time before making contact.

(There are several who help me in my research, though of course they are not aware that it is they themselves whom I study!)

As many ways as I have located the Affected, there is as

much variation among them. For, like the rest of us, they are individuals, and differ drastically, one from another. Some have little comprehension remaining—though in most cases the original intellectual capacities are impossible to determine—and others remain sharp, while adopting new fixations, or regressing to the fascinations of adolescence or even before. They develop new tastes in food, music or fashion. And there is the forgetfulness, the lost time, the erratic sleep patterns, the attempts at self-medication.

Again, specific examples of this range will follow—and at the same time as I attempt to account for this variation, I will strive to delineate some common features that may, taken together, serve to identify the Affected. Let me now, then, attempt a preliminary definition, with some cursory examination of causes and suggestion toward my hypotheses.

1. The Affected are those individuals who have been electrocuted almost to the degree of death, yet have not died. They have come close enough, however, that it may be said that they remain suspended (again, there is variation toward which pole they tend) between life and death.

2. These individuals retain a sensitivity to, and dependence upon electricity.

3. It has come to my attention that the wire involved in human electrocution is also transformed—that wire which has killed or shocked an individual to an Affected state pos-

sesses specific properties that may potentially be unlocked.

4. Furthermore, it is only the Affected who are able to gauge the transformation in this wire, and it is for this that I employ them, to differentiate and grade the wire so I may seek its potential.

Are there reasons beyond curiosity that have led me to develop these theories, to gather this body of knowledge and to conduct my experiments? Quite simply, yes. Money, I should say, is necessary, and one product of my search, but it is not an end. No. Knowledge—science, in a way—is what I am after, what I write for, what I hope to share. And this knowledge, it is also for myself. I will transport myself to a different way of life.

Might it be possible to attain the heights of their experience without suffering the drawbacks? To access what is most electric in us, most alive?

Answering these questions is akin to science, and also detective work, and has proved a compelling frustration. Much of the difficulty is caused by the one characteristic that all the Affected share:

5. The Affected have no insight into their condition, no awareness that they are different from other people or how they themselves were before their electrical incidents—in fact, they are unable to recall these incidents. You can explain the situation to their faces (I have tried, in fact, many times)

and they will never understand. They will react with disbe-lief, ridicule, and consternation. These are not people who can explain anything to you.

17.

THE AMUSEMENT PARK was almost a hundred years old. Oaks Park, right along the river, all its rides rickety and rattling, providing extra thrills—the Rock-O, the Tilt-A-Whirl, the Scrambler and the Looping Thunder, a roller coaster held together by duct tape and fear.

The three rode the Ferris wheel, on the far end of the park, taking it all in from the highest vantage point possible. Kayla sat in one basket with Leon, and Chris sat in the one in front of them; he kept turning around, checking for something. A sign on the back of his basket said DANGER! DO NOT ROCK SEAT! Fluorescent tubes of light stretched along the metal framework. Kayla knew Chris was afraid of heights, that he didn't like the thrill rides. The Ferris wheel was about all he could take.

"Look under our feet," she said to Leon, "it's the same grip tape as on a skateboard's deck."

"Yeah," Leon said. "It is. Look at all the people."

"Kiken no imi nanka shittemo inai ne."

"Whatever you say," he said.

"How are you feeling?" she said. "What are you thinking about?"

Leon didn't reply. The red sun was setting behind the west hills. The distant silhouettes of the buildings downtown looked fake. A tour boat plowed slowly up the river. Kayla looked down at the pathetic teenagers heading for the roller rink; she looked at the top of the carousel, how the round, orange rooftop was made to look like the top of a tent. As the Ferris wheel took them lower, she could see the horses and other gaudy animals slide past, rising and falling.

"Wait for a complete stop," a pre-recorded voice said.

They swept up, backward. Directly beneath them, whole fat families raced go-carts. Everyone ignored the miniature golf course. Kayla snorted at the sight of it. She wore a skirt, and leaned her leg against Leon's. He didn't seem to notice. Turning, she looked carefully at his face, the smooth skin, the slack, clueless expression, his hair still only a hint of bristles. After a moment, he felt her gaze and looked back at her.

"What?" he said. "Is that silver on your eyes?"

"Eyelids," she said. "It's glitter."

Above the screams and shouting, distant fireworks exploded. Leftover Black Cats and bottle rockets, out in the neighborhoods; tonight was the fifth of July. Leon turned farther, to look behind them, toward the sound.

Across the bracken, watery nature reserve, above the dead, drowned trees, a hundred-foot-tall great blue heron was painted on the wall of the crematorium.

"That's where they burn up dead people's bodies," Kayla said.

"I know."

"They hide the smoke, somehow," she said.

Kayla saw that Leon was not looking at the crematorium; instead, he focused on the thick power lines, the towers that stretched across the river. Atop some of the towers were platforms—Canada geese nested there, awkwardly coming and going. She had been watching Leon carefully, these past couple weeks, collecting clues. Direct questions had been the least successful; she had to follow wherever he wanted to go. Now he seemed impatient, his hands gently pounding the metal bar across their laps. As they descended the front of the wheel, his impatience increased; he bent forward to see under the carousel's roof as early as possible, to extend the length of his vision. Kayla did the same, watching the mostly empty horses, the saddled elephants and giraffes come leaping around.

"No rocking!" said the cigarette-voiced man operating the wheel, his puffy face flashing as they were pulled backward, underneath. "You, girl," he said, "you're the one I'm talking to." Already they were climbing away from him, back toward the top.

It seemed darker than when they first got on the ride; the plastic bracelets on her wrists were beginning to glow in the dark. The fluorescent lights were brighter, illuminating their dangling feet.

"Last night," Kayla said, "you know, Chris and I went to Forest Park and deposited the rest of the money, from Natalie. There's getting to be a lot of it."

"Good," Leon said.

"Good? Where were you?"

"Last night?" He looked up at the pale stars. "There's a lot going on," he said. "I lose track. I don't think I'm sleeping very much."

"You don't think so?" Kayla said. "Where were you?"

"I don't remember," he said. "My parents, man."

"What about them?"

"I don't even want to talk about it." He leaned forward again, straining to see under the roof of the carousel. "Holy crow," he said.

Kayla watched the whole painted menagerie—the horses, the ostriches, the lions and tigers—slide past. A few hyperactive children rode these beasts, and a couple who were afraid, their parents standing next to them. And then a grown man came into view, just as Leon exclaimed. The man's long thin legs were bent up; he rode a giant rooster. He turned his head and his black, pointed beard framed his face.

"What?" Kayla said. "What is it? Did you see someone?"

"No," Leon said. "I don't know. Nothing." He looked away, his eyes cutting sideways; he scratched at the side of his face.

"Once more around," the operator said, flashing by. "I'm watching you!"

They climbed, Chris in his basket right behind them, then directly above, then in front of them again. He stole a glance backward, checking, and turned to face forward. Almost immediately he spun toward them again, and pointed out over the park.

"There!" he said. "The sailor's down there. All the way over there by the Scrambler."

All Kayla saw was a figure sitting on a bench, and then the treetops, blocking her view.

"That fool?" she said. "Let's go see what he's doing."

"All right," Leon said, "if you guys want to."

Back on the ground, up close, everything was that much more pathetic. Fat women in terry cloth shorts with blurry tattoos on their calves, old guys with mustaches carrying combs in their back pockets, stupid plush animals, inflatable superheroes. Kayla saw how Leon slowed as they passed the carousel; the bearded man was nowhere to be seen. Chris trailed her, too, even though it wasn't easy walking in her tight skirt, her platform sneakers. She looked back at them, and noticed for the first time that now Chris was taller than Leon. That had happened since the beginning of the summer. She wondered whether to say anything.

"We could go through the haunted house," Chris said, "instead of the Looping Thunder."

"You wish," Kayla said. "It's boring—the black light,

the skeletons, the same haunted mill idea as every single haunted house, ever."

"People are looking at the way you're dressed," he said.

"If we were in Tokyo, no one would think a thing," she said.

"Exactly."

Teenagers, some of whom she recognized from school, strutted past, pretend-fighting, flirting. The three walked past the pink plastic slides, past the shooting gallery with the two piano players as targets. The most pathetic of all were the teenagers who worked at the park—tired-looking, smoking clove cigarettes, acting old. She didn't know how people could let themselves fall apart like that.

They passed the fun house mirrors at the entrance, toward the booth where people threw darts at balloons. And there, facing the Rock-O and the Tilt-A-Whirl, sat the sailor himself, Steven. He wore huge black sunglasses, even though it was dusk. He seemed to be asleep, he was so still. A stupid-looking dog rested next to him, on a short leash. It wore a red vest that said something on it in white letters.

"Now this is a sad sight," Kayla said.

–◠◠◠–

Steven listened to the ringing of the bell. It sounded like a train, a miniature train, which must run right behind the bench, on the other side of the low fence. He could feel the links of the fence with his fingers. He smelled cigarette smoke and popcorn. He could not see a thing. Around him, machinery groaned and gears whined, gnashing; this, combined with the screams, great waves of them, made it seem he was surrounded by a medieval torture chamber.

"Shoot the clown in the mouth! Right in the mouth! Win Scooby Doo!"

He listened, trying to imagine the people behind the voices. Reaching out, he felt Ross's bony, furry skull for reassurance. This was a test for both of them, and the dog sat up at Steven's touch, as if they might go somewhere. Steven was not yet ready for that attempt. He shivered, and imagined Heather hiding somewhere, spying on him—but of course that was impossible. She couldn't spy on anyone.

She had left him here; she said she would return. This was all her idea, and she had taken great care with his eyes. The preparations had taken almost an hour. First, coins, then bread dough, then oblong pieces of black leather that she carefully taped to his eye sockets. Finally, the black glasses with the sidepieces. With these glasses, and the cane, and the dog, anyone would think he was blind. And he was.

"How many tickets do you have?"

"You can't buy a corndog with tickets!"

"Why not?"

People appeared out of nothing, nowhere, and disappeared the same way, with the same completeness. Ross settled again, the heavy, steady shape of him against Steven's leg. Neither one of them was alone. Steven tried to concentrate, to be aware. The blind live in a world of time, not space—he'd heard this repeated so often, and yet he had no sense of how much time had passed. He might have been sitting here half an hour, or much longer. Or shorter. A skittering raced behind his head. A chipmunk, or a rat. And there was the clap of a pigeon's wings.

He wanted to take off the glasses, everything, and see what all this was, to unveil the mysteries; at the same time, he didn't want to, he wanted to remain caught in the confusion, to wallow in it. After all, sight only provided different mysteries, as Heather had pointed out.

"Mommy! You forgot what Keith said!"

A river of voices, of footsteps, flowed around him. And music somewhere, some damn Eagles song.

"You in the tube top," a man's voice whispered, "you like me…"

Steven had never been to the park before, though he'd passed it many times, out on the river. His houseboat had been docked nearby; he had no idea where the boat was now. These past few weeks, Heather had let him stay at her place—on the couch, at first, and then with her, in her bedroom.

He had imagined how it would be, with her restless hands all over his body, seeing him through touch, but when it happened, she seemed more distant than that. Perhaps his expectations got in the way, or his vision came between them, took them to two different places. Heather's body was so pale, so smooth. She was wider than he was; on top of her, looking down, he could see her left hip, and her right, on either side of him. At first, he couldn't help looking, and keeping the lights on, but lately he had been switching them off, closing his eyes. This seemed to help; at the very least, it kept him from seeing Ross at the foot of the bed, watching attentively, the dog ready to help if any assistance was needed, any signal given.

A trail of screams wheeled overhead, faded. Ross shifted against his leg. It was much more difficult to keep his mind from wandering, Steven realized, to keep himself in this place where he was. Distant from him, he heard young voices, a conversation he couldn't quite grasp.

"…a sad sight."

"What's he doing?"

"Stay back…"

"…people around…can't do…"

"…thunder, then…"

"All right."

Everything was starting to blur together, all the voices and music and machinery. The cane in his lap was made up of twelve-inch segments held together by an elastic cord that ran inside them. Its handle was like the grip of a golf club and the tapping of its hard tip let people know you were coming, and that you were blind. Now Steven unfolded the cane; Ross stood at the sound and, unsteadily, Steven did the same.

He shuffled, sliding the soles of his shoes; the cane would warn him, Ross would let him know if there were stairs, or any drop-off. He didn't trust them; the ground felt suspicious beneath him, as if it were conspiring to trick him. He kept on with the sense of others getting out of his way, close calls as reluctant children were pulled from his path. He crunched through spilled popcorn, felt the cold stickiness of a sno-cone against his bare arm. What if someone realized he wasn't actually blind? Would they be angry? What would he say? What if he encountered an actual blind person?

He tried to trust Ross. The dogs were not trained to work with the blind, the mantra went, they were *persuaded.* Steven did not find this distinction exactly reassuring. And now the smell of food—corndogs, hamburgers—thickened as he neared the snack counter; this he'd passed, on the way in, but now things would become more difficult, now he was not merely backtracking. As he walked, he felt the weight of stares—no one knew better than he, the guiltless satisfaction of staring at the blind, and now he realized how aware they might be. Ross led him gently on, the feeling of people slipping past on either side. He paused at the gentle, calm sound of a water fountain, gathered himself, then continued onward, through screams and gunshots. Someone leaned close to ask him if he wanted to throw a ball at something, then trailed off, not bothering to finish the offer.

He veered to the left, and felt a wooden edge, a table. He patted the air, slapped a bench, and sat down again.

"This area's reserved for birthday parties," a man's voice said. "Oh, excuse me, sir. Sit here for a while, if you like."

"Thank you," Steven said. "Could you tell me what time it is?"

"Five past eight."

Over an hour had passed; he wasn't certain if time was moving slowly or quickly. He felt exhausted and wondered how far he'd traveled. Probably not far at all; it was the mental effort translating into the physical weariness. Near his feet, Ross panted as if he, too, were tired. Around them, everyone shouted, no one spoke in lowered voices here.

"Skee ball!"

"Did you see me skate backward?"

"It's just a ball with mirrors stuck to it; they shine lights on it!"

Steven felt he should move, but also felt an inertia, a need to rest. He wanted to sit for at least five minutes, but had no way—outside of repeatedly asking passersby—of keeping this from sliding into half an hour or more. Suddenly, Ross's tail slid across the ground, slapping his ankle.

"Hey there, American," Heather said. She was close, perhaps sitting across the table.

"I thought we were supposed to meet at the bench at eight-thirty."

"Oh," she said, "did we have a plan together?"

"Heather?" he said.

"Have you forgotten what I look like? True, this black hair—but Denise Michele is Hawaiian, you know—"

"Natalie," he said. "I'm sorry."

"Don't be sorry."

"I'm blind," he said. "I mean I'm practicing being blind."

"For sympathy?" she said.

"No," he said. "Well, to help me understand. And I'm helping train this dog here, too."

He smelled the faint perspiration, the heat of her body as Natalie leaned closer. He flinched as she tapped at the lenses of his glasses with her fingernails.

"Yes," she said. "You're blinded, you sure are. Where have you been? When was the last time I saw you?"

"I don't know," he said. "It didn't seem like a good idea to be in touch again, after last time."

"Oh, yes," she said. "It just came back to me—I had a good time that night, don't worry; in fact, we could do it again. Eleven more times, if you want, and then we could go back through the months, or if you have a favorite—"

"No," he said. "I'm seeing someone. I don't think it's a good idea, but I appreciate it."

Natalie laughed. "You'd be surprised what a girl like Linda Beatty would do," she said. "I've been practicing my poses, wearing that striped towel like a turban on my head."

"Natalie," he said.

"Stop taking everything so serious," she said. "I'm kidding. It's all up to you."

"Are you riding the rides?" he said, trying to shift the conversation.

"What?"

"Here at the park."

"Oh, no," she said. "I have some work to do, here."

A man ran past, shouting about a family reunion. A wave of screams crested and faded away. It took a moment for Steven to realize that Natalie was no longer sitting with him, that she was gone. He tried to see if he could feel the absence, the empty space she'd occupied; he wasn't certain if he could tell a difference.

–∿–

Natalie walked quickly through the midway, away from the noise of the games and the rides, the shrieking and carrying on. The two-inch wooden soles of her brown sandals knocked on the asphalt path as she moved closer to the river, through the picnic sites, the sections of land that could be rented for gatherings. She passed emptied buckets of chicken, smoldering grills, groups of heavy, similar-looking people drinking beer from cans and smoking cigarettes. Someone whistled at her; she did not turn. The wide brim of her straw hat hid her eyes.

While the adults wasted the evening, she knew, the children ran to the amusement park. And when the money ran out, as darkness fell, the children would be left to their own devices, and they would find the fringes of the tended land, and stray down along the riverfront, into the bushes and thickets. Her pockets were full of girls—Patti and Hope, Laura, Linda and Ann, torn and stiffened, used and still eager, still free, so close to the Fourth of July—and she had to get them out, make them available.

A fat raccoon, dragging a bag of popcorn along the ground, entered the bushes just in front of her. Already the blackberry thorns snagged at her knee socks. She braided her hair before going any farther, then moved silently down the overgrown paths, into the hidden clearings, the settings for misdemeanors, for secrets. She slipped torn pages under bushes, in tall, dry grass. The girls smiled out; they snapped suspenders; they bathed; they stripped in roadside cafés. Someone would find them, some young girl would keep them. A glance would explain what all those fireworks were hinting at.

And then, a rustle, deep in the undergrowth. The bushes shook. Natalie stepped closer, pulled back a branch. A tall, gangly man wearing slacks, a white dress shirt, was crawling on all fours. He looked up at her, his pale face set off by his sharp, black beard. Had she seen him before?

"I don't know you," he said. "I'm not doing anything wrong."

"I don't know you, either," she said, letting go of the branch. She listened to the rustling fade as he crawled away in the other direction.

18.

THE DAY HAD DRAWN TO ITS CLOSE, the customers of Shanghai Shanghai long gone. Chesterton sat down and opened his notebook. Of his subject this evening, he wrote with great relish:

IV. ON VICTOR MACHADO

In this chapter I hope to reflect upon the character and examine the person of Victor Machado, the most dependable of those who work for me, the one among the Affected with whom I have developed what might be understood as a relationship.

Victor is a gangly, skinny, awkward fellow, his dark hair shorn close to his skull, his black beard tapering to a well-defined point. His speech is flustered and formal. He gives the impression of being constantly out of his depth. As to his height: he is only slightly shorter than I am, and I stand six foot nine inches in my stocking feet, my head held level.

Victor is a man whom I've studied in hopes, but with no certainty, that what I've learned can be extrapolated to others among the Affected population—or, ultimately, to the rest of us. And yet I hope to stress that he is a person, not merely a subject of study, that I have become fond of him. I must freely admit this, as it may influence the course of my investigation.

I look out for Victor, I look after him—I brush his teeth; I polish his shoes each morning, and send him out. I would cut his hair, if it needed it, or trim his handsome, striking beard, yet herein lies one mystery. Perhaps this is the one area where he cares for his appearance; perhaps, it has occurred to me, his hair simply does not grow.

I must digress to provide the necessary background. I did not seek out Victor; he found me. He came looking for employment. No one else would give him a job, what with the community notification laws that exist and every other thing.

Where to begin?

Victor Machado was electrocuted in 1998, on the rooftop of a private junior high school in Beaverton, Oregon. It is my belief that he had good reason to be on this rooftop, that he was working on the ventilation system or even checking for leaks against the coming winter rains. He was found in a narrow passageway where wires clustered, and he got tangled up. It could have happened to anyone. He was almost killed by the current that passed through him, and barely resusci-

tated. But this was only the half of Victor's misfortune—

—For the site where they found him was next to two rows of skylights: one looked into the girls' shower, while the other shone down into the boys' locker room. It could be argued that Victor had been spying on these students while they were undressed and washing themselves. What's more, the electrical shock that he underwent was sufficiently severe as to remove his very clothes from his body.

The fact of Victor's nakedness when discovered, along with his proximity to the young and unclothed, is what generated the charges against him, what ultimately led to the strictures and probation that now bind him.

I must pause here, I must again digress in order to discuss Victor's susceptibility to suggestion, what I would term his malleability. He is a fellow extremely prone to the influence of opinion, very eager to provide the desired reaction (as I have already demonstrated in my description of Walter, and others, such flexibility is not uncommon in the Affected; however, some rare individuals may be characterized by an unshakable fixity of purpose). I believe that Victor agreed to the false charges against him not out of actual guilt, but because such guilt was suggested to him and he could not resist the suggestion.

This young man is the most amenable among the Affected to experimentation, the gentlest by far. For instance, I once ordered a device from a newspaper advertisement, a simple set-up that promised to provide the growth and definition of one's muscles through the application of low-level *electrical impulses. This process was supposedly developed by the Russians and is known as Russian Stimulation or, more familiarly, Russian Stim. I did not find the device helpful, or interesting for my purposes, but recently—some years after procuring the device—I attempted to hook it up to Victor, to see how his body would react. I adhered the electrodes to his body, and the machine exploded before I'd even plugged it in!*

I get ahead of myself, and further discussion of this experiment and those of a much more advanced nature will follow. In this chapter I must focus on presenting the character and person of Victor Machado. Forgive me.

Of course, I am aware that the history above is my version of Victor's story, and I am no impartial observer. The possibility remains that this gentle fellow was a sex offender, a pervert, that I—no matter how much I protest—have it backward here. There is also the danger that his probation for child molestation, all the counseling he receives, might actually suggest such activity to him, bend him in this unfortunate direction. This is why strictness is necessary. It is necessary to keep him occupied.

Victor works for me. He is dependable, indispensable. He runs errands; he picks up the wire from the drop-off site; he helps me in the complicated process of melting the copper, molding the bracelets, anklets and the like. Still, I do not always have enough work to keep him busy at all hours (especially because he sleeps so little), so it is sometimes necessary to send him on scurrilous errands, just to keep him out of trouble. Scavenger hunts, almost—I send him out for a specific number of bottlecaps, for instance, a specific brand, found at a set location; I ask him to tell me what color cars are parked in front of a certain store on Burnside, that kind of thing.

I feel affection for him. If I didn't buy him new clothes, he wouldn't think to do so. I must put notes in his pockets— his memory is not strong—to remind him of his assignments and even my address. Every morning, I shine his shoes. Perhaps I mentioned that; allow me to add detail: he puts his foot up on a wooden box, and I polish the right shoe, then the left. They are pointed black wingtips, fine shoes. I look up and Victor is watching with fierce concentration.

Sometimes I think of stories I've read, near-hypothetical accounts of people found frozen in blocks of ice and somehow brought back to life, into a different world, and I think of Victor. His recoveries are manifold—emotional, physical (this is a fellow who had a toe grafted to his left hand, in place of the thumb lost in the accident), even intellectual.

And this bears on one of the primary foci of these, my written investigations of the lives of the Affected and what might be gleaned from them. Can these individuals learn? What do they make of the notion of progress? Do they aspire to it, or does repetition satisfy them in a way that we cannot imagine? I suspect that the answer may lie in a different relationship to time (might they live in a world that multiplies possibilities without the danger of time ever running out?), and my suspicions must await a later and certainly a more deliberate treatment.

19.

THE THREE STOOD ON THE CROWDED MAX platform at Lloyd Center, yet they did not stand together. Leon was fifty feet away—walking tight circles, clenching and unclenching his fists, his eyes apparently closed—and he did not realize that Chris and Kayla were watching, following.

"Let's just talk to him," Chris said.

"We've tried that a million times," Kayla said. "You know what we decided."

"What if he sees us?"

"We'll tell him we're going to Cal Skate," she said. "I need some new wheels, anyway; he can get some grip tape."

The sun shone down, late afternoon. Kayla wore her usual skate clothes, not the sandals and skirt and makeup. Chris chewed at his lip and looked past her; now standing between a man with a bicycle and two old ladies, Leon lifted his feet, eyes closed, and walked in place. Even at this distance, the collar of his T-shirt looked stiff, corrugated, as if he'd been chewing on it and it had dried that way.

"Train," Kayla said.

The brakes whistled and whooshed; the doors jerked open. People poured out, swinging shopping bags, wheeling bicycles. Leon disappeared into the front car.

Chris and Kayla got in the next one back, sitting where they could see Leon through the two windows, so they would know where he got off, and could follow. Doors closed, the MAX slid west, through traffic, toward the river, downtown. Leon faced away from them, oblivious; he stood with both arms stretched over his head, hanging on.

Soon they were crossing the Steel Bridge—below, the river stretched black and blue; a jet-ski tore its surface; a boat with a ragged sail struggled upwind.

"Look," Kayla said. "The sailor's girlfriend."

Four seats ahead, a tall, strong-looking woman sat in a black skirt, a white blouse, and dark glasses. She held a slender white cane with a red tip between her feet, its handle pointing at the ceiling.

"She can hear us," Chris said, whispering. "Probably. They can hear a long way."

"Watch this," Kayla said. Standing, she stepped down the aisle, sitting down across from the blind woman. She reached out and touched the woman's shoulder.

"Excuse me," she said. "We're almost downtown. Just so you know."

"I realize that," the woman said. "I know where I am."

"Do you need any help?" Kayla said.

"No, thank you. I'm headed to an important appointment."

Chris listened and watched, also trying to keep track of Leon. If Leon looked back and recognized him, he would wave. He would talk to him, again, try. In a way, he wished he were in the other car, his arm around Leon's shoulder, just being his friend.

"Can I ask you a question?" Kayla was saying to the blind woman.

"Yes."

"I'm afraid it might be a little rude."

Chris leaned forward, his neck against the seat in front of him, listening. Outside, the buildings of downtown slid past, people on the sidewalks, cars on every side.

"Go ahead," the blind woman said.

"That cane, does it fold down?"

"Yes, it does."

"Can I see it?" Kayla said. "I mean, hold it?"

The doors opened, the voice overhead saying "Pioneer Courthouse Square."

"Kayla!" Chris said. "Leon!" He pulled on her arm as the doors opened, as people pushed their way in and out.

They slipped through the crowd, the two of them, past the Starbucks, the red bricks beneath their feet, the fountain and all the people—the hippies with clipboards, petitions to save trees or owls; the businessmen in suits and ties; the fake punk rockers and heroin-addict wannabes, kids in vinyl trench coats leading others on leashes, their spiky hair, their pimply necks. Where was Leon?

There, moving away from them, jaywalking, his face upturned as if he were asleep.

Chris and Kayla set after him, walking parallel, on the other side of the street. West to east: Fifth, Fourth, Third Avenues. They dodged through traffic. Cars honked. A bus driver shouted something.

"You stole that?" Chris said.

Kayla looked down, and laughed, surprised to see the blind woman's white cane, still in her hand. Hardly slowing, she bent, then collapsed the cane; it telescoped in on itself until it was only a foot long.

The trees' green leaves snapped overhead, and smokers clustered in doorways, and one-legged pigeons hopped out of the way. South to north: Stark, Oak, Pine Streets. It wasn't hard to keep up with Leon—he was barely lifting his feet from the cobblestones, sliding his shoes along, his arms limp at his sides—and it was easy not to be seen, as he only looked straight ahead, focused, his expression unchanging. They crossed Burnside, near the red gate to Chinatown.

"Look behind him," Chris said. "Who's that? Abraham Lincoln?"

Halfway down the block, a tall, bearded figure moved jerkily along, his serious face suspended above the heads of everyone on the sidewalk around him. He, too, seemed to be following Leon.

"I think maybe I've seen him before," Chris said.

"At Oaks Park?"

"No, I don't think so. I can't remember."

"You sound like Leon," Kayla said. "Leon knows him, I think. Maybe. Or something."

"Look where he's going—"

Leon had turned down a narrow alley, and the man followed; both moved more quickly, now, shambling with purpose. Kayla was already after them, Chris close behind. They could no longer see Leon, only the man, who did not look back.

Toward the end of the alley, before it dead-ended, a green dumpster stood. The man disappeared behind it, around the far side.

"Come on," Kayla said, whispering.

High overhead, windows were covered by bars and dirt. Rusted fire escapes dangled from the brick walls; fans blew smoke and grease from restaurant vents.

The man did not reappear. Kayla and Chris stood ten feet from the green dumpster. After a moment, she bent down and looked along the ground, the space beneath the dumpster, out the other side.

"He's gone," she said, whispering. "I can't see his feet."

"Maybe he climbed inside there, somehow," Chris said.

Kayla took hold of his arm and pulled him forward, toward where the man had disappeared.

Around the far side of the dumpster was a manhole, its cover half slid off, a dark moon of bottomless space in the gap.

"They went down there," Chris said.

"Obviously." Kayla bent down and pushed at the cover. "Help me."

The cover slid across with a gristly, scraping sound. A damp wind rose from the round hole, blowing in their faces. A thin ladder stretched down, only the first few rungs visible.

Kayla turned; she descended slowly, into a concrete vault. Wires snaked in and out of boxes, all along the walls.

"Telephone lines, there," she said, low, to herself. She lifted her hands just before Chris stepped on them.

At the bottom of the ladder, the space opened, darkness all around. Light filtered down, barely; their eyes adjusted as much as they could. Their feet kicked up dust; the air smelled dirty, stale.

"Where?" Chris said.

"Shh," she said, her hand over his mouth.

Slowly, they began walking, following one wall into the darkness. Shards of glass cracked beneath their feet. Overhead, pipes suddenly loomed, everywhere, thick and narrow, dripping and dusty dry. Pressure gauges flashed round and white like the faces of clocks. The brick walls were uneven; here and there were holes, like rough doorways made by sledgehammers. Kayla and Chris leaned against each other; they held hands.

The air did not seem like air—thicker, greasier; it hummed, it tasted like metal in her mouth, deep in her throat as she swallowed. She heard footsteps overhead, then they were gone. A slant of light angled from a cracked floorboard overhead, and winked away; a glow from a forgotten trouble lamp hooked down some bent passageway. The dark tightened. Were there other people, movements around them? Rats? The two stood still for a moment, and so did everything else.

Chris tugged on Kayla's arm; the man's long shape jerked close by, suddenly, then moved away, after something else—Leon?

They stumbled, trying to keep up. Kayla telescoped out the blind woman's cane, feeling their way along. She lost track of the man in the darkness, as it thickened around them. Were they descending farther? The broken-down tunnel opened into an underground room, into a larger cavern, narrowed to another broken-down tunnel. Here and there, shafts of pale light, stripes of dust, slanted down.

Kayla felt Chris's damp hand on her face, turning her head to see. There, just across the tunnel, the bearded man stood—pressed flat against a wall, a white moth, his arms outstretched. Slowly, he moved, sliding along, another twenty feet down the tunnel, then pressed himself against the wall again. He continued to proceed in this manner, and they followed, cautiously, at a distance.

The man seemed to be working at something, bending a piece of the wall with his hands. His white shirt made him look like a masked ghost, his beard hiding the edges of his face. Then, without warning, he slipped away, inside the wall somehow, leaving them there.

Kayla pulled Chris across the tunnel; a piece of plywood, only visible up close, leaned against the brick wall. She bent it out and they could see the rough hole in the bricks, the space through which the man had gone, where Leon had to be.

On hands and knees, Kayla went first. The ceiling was close above her head. She could not tell how far the man was ahead of her; she could not see him. Crawling, she slowed and Chris slapped the bottom of her shoe, bumping her. She let go of the cane, left it behind, pulled herself along. And then there was light ahead, a door being opened, a fresh gasp of air tinged by spices. Kayla hurried; she heard Chris breathing behind her and tried to hold her breath, not to make a sound.

When she reached the trap door, she waited, slowly looking up, expecting the man to be looking down at her. She could see nothing about the room overhead except the fluorescent lights, flickering in the ceiling.

"Not now, Victor!" a man's deep voice said. "I'm quite busy at this moment."

Kayla hesitated, Chris close behind her. Slowly, she raised her head, just enough so her eyes were at the height of the floorboards. She saw no one, nothing except shelves, aisles; it was some kind of shop. Quickly, she slid out of the tunnel, down an empty aisle. Chris followed, crawling sideways.

"This day is so long," said another man's voice—he paced across the room, and Kayla saw that it was the bearded man. "I'm only trying to be helpful," he said, "you know, certainly, and I came here to see—"

Kayla and Chris slid farther toward the shop's dim corner. A row of dusty cardboard boxes was stacked near the wall, a narrow space there to hide, gaps to see through; they were ten feet from the men, yet could not be seen. Here, the smell of spices thickened. The signs on the wall were in Chinese or Korean; Kayla could not quite make sense of them. She leaned around the aisle, still low, just enough to see the other man, who was turning the sign in the window from OPEN to CLOSED, locking the front door. This man was even taller than the first one, and built more solidly. His head was up near the ceiling, and bald; the fluorescent lights reflected along the angles of his skull as he turned. His skin dark black, his face serious, he looked like a retired basketball player; he walked stiffly, hardly bending his knees, his long arms swinging straight. He stepped closer. He did not see them.

"You must remember, Victor," he said, "to close this trap door. There's a draft, on top of everything else. Now, now—that's not a reprimand, simply a fact—"

He put his arm around the bearded man and they walked across the room, beyond where Kayla could see. She turned and looked at Chris, his frightened face, his mouth open; he had also been watching the man. Kayla winked, but still Chris stared, afraid, his eyes strained, a nerve ticking in his neck. On the shelf next to him were dried mangos in jars, and folding fans; silver, dried fish stared out through cellophane bags.

"Where's Leon?" he mouthed, and Kayla shook her head, trying to calm him.

"I forgot something," the bearded man was saying. "Something I was doing. Underground. I lost—what?—"

"Of course you did," the other man said. His shiny black shoe was close enough that Kayla could have reached out and touched it. She held her breath.

"I forgot, I forgot, I forgot." The man hopped slightly, repeating himself.

"Don't fret about that, Victor. Listen to me—I would like for you to take the train out past the zoo. Bring me a stalk of Queen Anne's lace from a ditch in Beaverton."

"Very good."

"Also, Victor, I would like a matchbook from the Bagdad Theater on Hawthorne, and a leaf from a tree on the corner of Alberta Street and Northeast Eighth Avenue. I'll write it down for you."

"Excellent."

The two men walked together, back across the shop, away from Chris and Kayla. The black man pulled the trapdoor open again, and the bearded man climbed into it; saying nothing more, he was gone.

The black man closed the trapdoor with an expression of satisfaction. He unrolled a carpet across the floor where the door was hidden, then looked around the store before fixing his attention on a bookcase behind the cash register. Stiffly, he walked toward it.

Kayla shifted to see better, and heard Chris do the same, behind her. The man took down a notebook, opened it on the counter next to the cash register, and seemed to read what was written there. Then, a feathered quill in his hand, he began to write. In front of him were displays of copper bracelets; pieces of jade, lacquered boxes. Everything around him looked small, fragile. The counter shook slightly as he wrote. He smiled, enjoying himself, pausing to choose the right words.

And then there was a tapping at the window next to the front door, a rhythm, a kind of code. The man leapt up, knocking his leg on the counter. He hopped and limped around to the door, passing close by where Kayla and Chris were hidden, fishing out a huge ring of keys.

The last person through the door was the blind woman from the MAX.

"Heather," the man said. "Nice to see you. And whom have you brought along?"

The sailor, Steven, stepped in next. He wore dark glasses, also, and held a white cane, acting as if he were blind. He felt his way along with his hands, shuffled his feet. He looked even more pathetic than usual—a foot shorter than the black man, not even as tall as the blind woman.

Kayla fought off a sneeze; Chris was pressed even closer to her now, watching, his head above her own.

"You said it would be all right, Mr. Chesterton," the blind woman said.

"Absolutely. The process does require two people."

"My name's Steven," the sailor said, holding out his hand at the wrong angle, as if he could not tell how tall the man was.

The black man, Chesterton, didn't shake it. "Very well," he said. "Come along."

Reaching out, he took hold of Heather's arm and Heather grasped Steven's hand; the three of them, linked, moved toward the back of the shop. There, they turned and began climbing a partially hidden staircase.

"Hurry," she said, hissing at Chris.

"What about Leon?" Chris said, whispering. "Is he in here?"

"Still in the tunnel, probably."

They looked at each other, each wondering if Leon was lost beneath them, each thinking of the bearded man's pursuit.

Chris pointed toward the trapdoor. "Let's find him."

"This can help us, maybe," Kayla said. "All of this, about what's happening with him. We have to find out what we can."

"But Leon—"

Kayla pulled Chris out of the hiding place, closer, where it was not safe to talk. They could hear the creak of footsteps, climbing. She peered around the corner, then nodded; the stairs were clear. Before climbing, though, she pointed at her shoes, then Chris's. They bent down and unlaced them with trembling fingers; they continued upward in stocking feet.

Halfway up, Kayla paused. She could see the back of the sailor's head—he was in the rear—moving down a hallway. The black man was explaining something, but she could not make out the words. She strained her neck, her ears. She felt Chris's breath on her bare arm. She kept moving. When they reached the top of the stairs, the hallway was empty. They passed an open doorway, a small room with its walls covered in maps. They slowed, but did not stop; they were crouched low, though it made no difference. The second door in the hallway, the last one, was closed. Kayla leaned her head against it and could hear sounds within—footsteps, low voices, the shifting of chairs or something metal. The only voice she could make out was Chesterton's, deep and commanding:

"Beware distractions, noises outside, any physical sensation. You will feel as if your heart is speeding up to an incredible rate. Do not worry."

The door had no keyhole; the slot for the key was right in the doorknob, tight, impossible to see through. Again, there was the sound of bodies shifting, of mumbled replies. Again, Chesterton's deep voice:

"There is no metal on your bodies? Remove your watch, sir. No, don't tell me your name again—I'm already trying to forget it. That's only a complication. Just take off all your clothes. Yes, that's right, that's right."

Kayla heard belt buckles, coins in pockets, the soft, heavy collapse of clothes dropped to the floor. Now Chris pressed his ear to the door, so he could listen. His face was inches from hers, his eyes open but not really looking. The metal sounds eased for a moment, and then there was a sound like claws across a hardwood floor, and further instructions:

"I have to slick down your hair with this—it makes your scalp more accessible and conductive, yes. It will be cold at first; it will warm up. Now, now you must breathe slowly. Concentrate. Listen to yourself breathe. Imagine your breath coming up through the soles of your feet, up your legs. Pull the energy through you. Try to imagine your hands are inside your legs, just inside the front of your torso, pulling up with your breath—"

Kayla looked at Chris; he stared back at her.

"I won't be in the room with you the entire time," Chesterton was saying. "Only for the sake of safety, to this point, only insofar as it is necessary. And now, as you continue, I will take my leave."

Suddenly, footsteps approached the door, growing louder on the other side. Chris and Kayla spun, bumping each other, sliding down the hallway, hands slipping against the walls, then onto the stairs, half-falling to the bottom.

They overran their shoes, then twisted to snatch them up, regaining their balance. Chris was ahead now; they darted beneath the fluorescent lights. The ceiling itself shook, a thumping overhead as if the people in the room had multiplied and were dancing. The lights rattled; dust rained down. Trailing, Kayla veered toward the counter. She clapped the open notebook shut on the quill pen and slipped the whole thing inside her shirt, almost running into Chris as he worked the key, the ring luckily still hanging in the front door's lock—

And then they were out on the sidewalk, still carrying their shoes, stumbling in the sunlight, startled, not looking back. They did not speak, right away; they passed under the red gate of Chinatown, back across Burnside.

"We couldn't find Leon, even if we tried," Kayla said.

"He went down there like he wanted to," Chris said, "like he'd been there before. Maybe he knew his way around. No one would catch him."

"It'll be all right," Kayla said, "We'll talk to him later. We will."

They walked close together, toward Pioneer Square, convincing each other.

Half an hour later—back on the MAX, the trip to Cal Skate put off to another time—Chris took from his pocket what he'd stolen from the store's shelves. The sign had said it was a dried monkey claw, but upon close inspection it was revealed to be fake, cleverly constructed of rabbit fur and wire. Kayla did not mention the notebook; she kept it concealed inside her shirt, its sharp edges against her skin.

20.

STEVEN SHIVERED. He swallowed, and felt the wire that circled his throat, the weight of the cold metal plate on his chest. He was still blind—the dark glasses, the tape, the dough, the coins pressed against his closed eyelids; Heather did not trust him to act blind without this; she feared he'd give himself away. She was close. He could hear her breathing, to his left. She had brought him here. This was something, she said, that only a few in the blind community knew about—a secret passed along, not to be repeated, a mysterious waiting list, a call that came out of nowhere. A call from the man with the deep voice: Chesterton.

Only now was Steven certain that he and Heather were alone, that this Chesterton had left the room. Only now did he dare lift his hands and touch the metal plate on his chest, follow the thin wires that radiated out from it; other wires were attached to his ankles, his wrists, all stretching away from him.

He reached out his arm, and his fingertips touched skin. Heather. The wires were attached to her, as well, connecting her to him. Just as he touched her, she began to laugh, and then to speak.

"The white lights are so bright!" she said. "I can see them, and I can see the woman—"

"What?" Steven said, turning his face in her direction, unable to see. Heather's voice was low, full of wonder, the words coming slow.

"—and she has long, blond hair, almost white, coming through a door, wearing boots that look like snake or crocodile skin. Green, green and yellow triangles. All the colors! She's throwing her white jacket on the floor. The boots are all she's wearing, her skin shines—oh, and a gold chain, a thin necklace, and she's tossing her hair around her shoulders, I can see her walking to a golden wicker chair, its wide back like a fan. There are white stockings on the floor, a garter belt, red, dark red cowboy boots, but she walks right past them—"

Heather laughed in surprise, in delight. The wires pulled on Steven, physically but inside, as well, as if sharp threads were being unwound, stripped out of his memory.

"—to a tall mirror on a stand, I can see it," Heather was saying, "and there's a hat, gray, hanging on the mirror, and other clothes, and now she's posing with the hat on her head, naked, cocking her hip, looking at herself in the mirror, having a great time, swinging the clothes around.

Her fingernails are so long and curved and so dark red. Wait! There's someone else in the mirror, someone behind her. It's a man—he's just standing there, nervous by the door, watching like he doesn't know what to do. He's trying to untie his shoes, his scalp shows through his red-dish, thinning hair. He's clumsy! His pants are off, now. He's a little paunchy—but all the lights are on the woman, and she's climbing onto the bed, grabbing its metal frame—"

A car honked somewhere. Steven heard the slap of Heather's hand on the floor, felt the pull of wire; he turned his head and the tape across his left eye popped free; the coin—a Susan B. Anthony dollar—bounced on the linoleum floor, and he reached up, straining against the wires, and pulled off his dark glasses, the tape and dough over that eye. Heather was still talking, facing the ceiling; she was naked except for the metal plates and wires, as was he. The copper plate on her chest was square, rectangular, while his was triangular. Shallow abrasions marked her wrists, her ankles, her neck. Suddenly she lifted up, on her hands and feet, moving like a crab to the end of the cot and back, wires sawing the air, tugging at him, and then she collapsed, flat on her back again. Her dark glasses slid off; she turned toward him, smiling, her white eyes wide.

"Heather," he said.

"Oh, it's sad," she said. "It's funny. I can see, I can see her on the bed, still in her boots and the sheets are pink, and there's a fur, gray and brown and black like a wolf, and she has a choker of shiny black beads around her neck, now. She's pausing, she's posing, stretching out across the bed, and she's pulling on a bright red, sheer blouse, then one of white lace, and she's gesturing for the man, the one in the doorway. She's saying something. He's repeating it—a name. *Patricia*? He reaches out and touches her, he's wearing bright white underpants, that's all, but he can't do it, doesn't dare. He's afraid. She's crawling across the bed, stretching up on her knees, but he's turned away, stumbling, gathering up his clothes—"

Steven lay still, watching and listening. The way Heather was talking, the way her legs and arms jerked, it seemed that the wires must be plugged into a socket somewhere. They were not. From what he could see of the room, there were only the two cots, and the rest was white—white metal cabinets, white linoleum floor, white blinds over the windows. He watched with his one eye, he listened to Heather. He'd never told her about the night with Natalie, the scene she was recounting. He hadn't told anyone; he had tried to forget it. Now his face was hot, a wave of confused shame passing over him, and at the same time he realized that Heather could not possibly recognize the woman she was describing as Natalie, that she did not even know that he himself was the man she was seeing, however she was seeing him.

Heather had stopped talking, stopped moving. The room was silent, only the faint tap and slide of wires as they settled.

Steven sat up, knelt on the hard floor next to her. She was breathing; she seemed to be asleep. He touched her forehead, her cheek, lifted the wires where they were tight. It was easiest to untwist them from his chest plate, his wrists and ankles. Loose, he stood and stretched. He had raw circles around his wrists, ankles; he felt the sharp line against his neck when he turned his head.

He could hardly remember agreeing to this, taking off his clothes, putting all this on. His hair was stiff, some kind of gel plastering it down. Stumbling, he lifted the dusty blinds away from the window. Pigeons clapped their wings, scattering from the rusted fire escape. He was on the second floor; below, on the sidewalk, people walked under a pale sun. SILVER DRAGON INC., one sign read; JAPANESE HAPPY FAST BOWL, said another. A red banner hung from a lamppost: CHINATOWN. He could see the edge of the tall red gate that spanned the street, next to a square yellow sign for CINDY'S THE ADULT BOOKSTORE.

He turned, shivering, and saw his clothes carefully folded to one side, almost as if they'd been laundered. How much time had passed? He pulled dough from his eyebrow, and began to dress before realizing how fast he was moving, how much he was depending on sight—

He misbuttoned his shirt. He dropped a sock behind a chair. He sat down on the cot again. He tried to hold in his breath, to exhale slowly, to rein in his heart. He felt not only exhausted, but also strangely exhilarated.

Footsteps approached. Steven fumbled for the dark

glasses; he got them back on his face just as the door opened and Chesterton entered. The size of the man was surprising, and his color, but not the formality with which he carried himself, the slight sadness—it went along with the tone and diction of his speech.

Chesterton paused; his gaze settled all around the room. He seemed slightly startled to see Steven dressed, but not upset.

"I trust," he said, "that her story all sounded very familiar to you, sir."

Heather stirred at the sound of his voice. She pushed herself up to a kneeling position, the copper plate pressing down on her breasts. She moved calmly, wearily. Chesterton set her folded clothes in front of her.

"Ah yes," he said. "I'm sorry—it seems like you had quite a time."

"Amazing," Heather said, her voice soft and distant.

"Perfect. Your sock, sir."

Steven was careful not to reach for it as the man held the sock out to him.

"How long since you've had vision?"

"Pardon me?" Steven said.

"How long have you been blind?"

"Well," Steven said, "I'm kind of like Heather. I'm still going."

"So you can remember."

"Yes; some things."

Chesterton was turned away, sideways, out of propriety, not watching Heather as she dressed. It made Steven like him more. He himself wanted to help her untwist the copper wires, help her dress—her skirt was inside out—but he did not.

"And you can see light and dark?"

"Not today."

Chesterton waved a huge hand in front of Steven's face, stopping just short of striking him. Steven held still; he did not flinch.

"Fantastic," Heather said, almost completely dressed. Her skirt was straight now; she'd turned it inside in. "It was so vivid. I saw—"

"That's fine. That is sufficient. I do not require this knowledge."

Chesterton bent down, pocketed the coin on the floor, then looked around the room one more time. Satisfied, he moved closer to take hold of Heather's arm, then Steven's, just above the elbow. He helped them to their feet, then led them through the door. Slowly, they passed down the hallway, the stairs.

They descended into the shop, which they had quickly passed through, earlier. How long ago? Steven felt his watch, heavy in his pocket, but couldn't take it out and check it. He was lucky, he realized, that Chesterton hadn't commented on the fact of his watch before; perhaps he had—perhaps he already suspected Steven of having vision, and that explained all the questions.

In the shop, small jade carvings were displayed next to

a shelf of copper bracelets not too unlike some of the things he and Heather had worn upstairs. Steven fought an urge to turn his head, to look around himself; he curled his toes inside his shoes and closed his one eye tight, felt the eyelid of the other, the flat pressure of the coin. He smelled incense, dirty cinnamon.

"Very fine," Chesterton said. "Thank you. That will conclude our work for today. I do appreciate your time, and trust that you found this an enlightening experience. I assure you that your pleasure is reciprocated." His voice dropped lower, his tone solemn and serious as he continued. "I need not remind you, of course, that you have agreed not to discuss this experience, to take it away with you. Not with other people, not even between yourselves when you are alone."

"Of course," Heather said. "We understand."

Chesterton led them to the door and turned the crowded key ring that hung there.

"Was this door unlocked?" he said, speaking to himself, shaking his head, and then he again took hold of Steven and Heather, guiding them out onto the sidewalk, gently into the stream of walking people.

21.

V. CONTINUED PRELIMINARY REFLECTIONS

I pause now from my description of Affected individuals, a task to which I will shortly return, in order to reflect on my motivations and methods, to suggest where I am headed, where I hope to arrive. A pause to catch my breath, a moment to check my feet, to be certain that they're beneath me.

Already the metaphors gather, when what I desire is to speak plainly, to present the facts. Here—this is how I've begun: after the wire is collected, after it is graded, I melt it down. This is the high-grade wire, wire involved in human electrocution, as previously defined. I melt and shape it into anklets, bracelets, chest plates, arm cuffs, and attach them to the naked bodies of two participants.

This works best with two people; to work with only one, it is more difficult to close the circuit—a phrase which I use only partially as a figure of speech—and to work with more than two individuals is something I cannot yet even consider. There is danger involved, the possibility of taking someone too far, of running them all the way down; of course, I can't anticipate every danger. My experiments are a way of demarcating the limits of safety.

I have forged copper plates for the solar plexus, and the hips; I have formed special bracelets and anklets—and in all these are holes through which wires are run, and it is by these wires that the two individuals are physically connected, and through them that deeper linkages occur. How to explain it, or suggest where these demonstrations will lead? Once connected in this manner, the one is infused somehow by the other (and vice-versa?).

I carefully select those on whom I experiment. The Affected? No; not yet; this I still consider. I must understand them better, first—they are not untrustworthy, merely inscrutable. The things they do, the reflection and self-consciousness that escapes them. For instance, they don't talk about the underground, don't recognize each other, or seem to. It's somehow shameful, perhaps, or there's a kind of code of conduct, but it's more likely that such memory is impossible for them. Perhaps there are those among the Affected who can remember their actions, or have some glimmering suspicions, who are trying to understand this phenomenon just as I am. This gives me hope.

So far I have concentrated on linking two UnAffected individuals, and studied the connections established between them through the medium of this wire. Cleverly, I have chosen to work among the blind—an almost arbitrary choice, at first made in a desire for secrecy, a wish not to be seen. The surprising, unexpected benefit that the process returned or provided visual memories to the blind—this maintains their desire to participate. I gather these people's recollections (secreted away in the adjoining room, I record it all through hidden microphones), in the interest of rigor, yet the usefulness of this material is dubious, or at the very least currently escapes me.

To return to my primary thrust: It has long been my suspicion that a different level, or perhaps quite different kind of experience (or action) takes place in the lives of the Affected. Does the belief in an ecstatic expansion, a positive experience or insightful other angle logically follow, when pursuing an understanding of the Affected, whose external lives are marked by so much dullness and repetition? Not necessarily. Here, I am convinced only by intuition.

I will be more myself, stepped up and wound tight, humming, my mind relentless, my body anticipating where I need to be. Will I be in this world, or another? Will clocks hold me, will I be in more than one place in a moment? It is too soon to say. These are only glimmerings, hot suggestions. My logic rattles, here, I realize; it is my hope that in retrospect the gaps in my reasoning will be filled, self-evident, that so much of what I am now eager to convince you, to convince myself, will shortly be plain—what appears preposterous will become familiar, unexceptional.

It may fairly be asked why I have not yet included myself

in the experiments; to this, I would respond that:

1. I don't wish to cloud my objectivity.

2. I am awaiting further results.

3. I have not yet met the ideal partner.

It may also be asked why I have not linked the Affected, but those who have carefully followed my argument probably fear this possibility in the same intrinsic fashion that I do. I fear this attempt would be foolhardy, catastrophic. To link an Affected individual with one who is UnAffected? I do not know. I have considered such a thing; I have considered linking my own body with Victor's. I hold out this possibility, I put it off. A last resort whose failure would leave me bereft, had I no other options.

I must proceed scientifically, not leap and lurch after my desires. In this way, perhaps, my desires themselves may change. I must better tune my instruments, better calibrate my experiments.

It was before dawn. Kayla sat alone at the skatepark under the Burnside Bridge, reading Chesterton's notebook, which she kept folded inside her own. As she read, she wrote questions, recorded her own thoughts. Some sections she read twice, three times; she did not allow herself to turn a page until she had understood. She paused longest over the diagrams—the dark lines that were copper wires, stretched from body to body, attached through copper plates, the people flat on their backs, faces hastily sketched in, eyes two black pinpricks, staring out at her.

She would take it all further, interpret things more clearly than Chesterton could, her mind less clouded; though she was quite taken by the logic and language of his writing, she also suspected it. After all, he was an adult, and adults deluded themselves in every direction.

She checked around herself, careful of discovery. It was gray, rainy, and the air smelled of wet ashes, some homeless campfire nearby. Atop the chain-link fence, a line of crows was perched, folding and unfolding their wings for balance. Kayla bent her neck back and looked up at the bridge's black underside, the whole thing trembling slightly, shaken by the cars and trucks she could hear but couldn't see. Then she looked back into the notebook, reading. *To access what is most electric in us, most alive.* She thought of Leon, as she read, and also of Natalie. As she had suspected, Leon was onto something, whether he realized it or not. And that was the question: how to get there. She too wanted to live another, better way, and in the stolen notebook she knew she had a key.

She closed the notebook's pages, buried it deep in her backpack. She tightened her shoelaces, took off her hoodie so she could skate in just a T-shirt—she'd given up all the Japanese clothes, that whole idea, since finding the notebook. That had been a dead end, connected to nothing, though she did not blame herself for following the possibility.

Standing, kicking her board around, she dropped in, down the six-foot wall, and rolled across the flat, concrete expanse, hard and gray and worn shiny, up the other side, around and around without pause, circling, tightening. She had grown bored with how everyone was skating, these days. Guys, mostly. It was all one big trick and then out—no sense of flow, foresight, any continuity. It was all about getting your picture taken, impressing someone, more about a moment than a feeling. Pathetic.

She ran a 50-50 grind along the near side of the bowl and saw him, standing up by her pack, watching. Leon. She carved up the far wall, gaining the momentum to pop up next to him without kicking again. He stood there with his hands in the pockets of his jeans, his face expressionless, his shoes untied.

"Where's your board?" she said.

"Forgot it, I guess. I thought you were a guy."

"I don't skate like a guy."

"No, not your skating," he said. "Your hair."

Kayla ran her hand across the stubble—smooth in one direction, rough in the other. The barber had tried to talk her out of it, but she had made him take it all the way down.

"I skate better than a guy," she said. "Different."

"I never saw a girl without hair before."

"Natalie."

"She's not a girl," he said, "and she wears wigs, most of the time."

"I like the feel of the wind," Kayla said. "I'm not wearing wigs or hats."

"Or helmets."

"Exactly."

As they spoke, Kayla paid careful attention to Leon. He seemed upset, perhaps, distracted, like he wanted to say something but couldn't figure out how. Or maybe that was just her, thinking he had something to tell her, hoping.

"You can take some runs on my board," she said.

"No, thanks."

"You all right?"

"I don't know."

"Why not?"

"Sleepy, maybe."

He glanced past her, and she turned to see a stray dog scuttle past, down an alley. As she looked away, she was thinking: *And then there is the forgetfulness, the lost time, the erratic sleep patterns, the attempts at self-medication* She turned back to Leon, and he looked at her as if he were a long way away, somewhere she could not go or reach. He was not trying to trick her, she reminded herself; just as the notebook had warned, he actually had no clue.

"It's just," he said. "It's just—forget it."

"Maybe I can help you," she said.

"No one can. I don't know what to do; I can't tell what's happening to me."

She kicked her board around in a gradual semicircle, uncertain how far to go. "Listen, Leon, I have some idea, I can tell you. It started the night of the accident, when you fell."

"What?"

"And it probably has something to do with Natalie," she said. "Are you doing things with her? Is she the problem?"

"It's not her; it's my parents—"

"Don't you see," Kayla said, "how it's all connected? You have to let me try to help—me and Chris."

Again, Leon was looking past her.

"What is it?"

"I thought I saw someone," he said.

"Where?" Kayla turned, squinting down the street—the alleys, dumpsters, parked trailers. "I don't see anyone."

"I guess not."

"Did you pierce your ears?" she said. "Why?"

"I didn't," he said. "They've always looked like that."

Kayla could see the tiny holes, the indentations, but she didn't argue. She sat down on her board, her knees bent, and rolled side to side, looking up at Leon.

"Can't you just tell me?" she said.

"Tell you what?"

"I'm your friend, Leon. I'm going to go where you go."

It was as if he didn't hear her, and it was the most important thing she had to say to him. Eyes wide, he looked like a frightened boy and then, in the same moment, like a young man who had seen something great or terrible. Kayla could only pick at the heels of her Chuck Taylors, where the canvas was unraveling. Their rubber toes were worn smooth and shiny from falls.

"Just tell me what you want to tell me," she said.

"You're just like them—questions and questions and questions; I don't even know what they're asking about."

"Who?"

Leon just looked at her as if she should know, as if he had told her.

After a moment, he said, "I'll see you later on?"

Kayla watched as Leon turned away and dropped down to the sidewalk. He shuffled out from the shadow of the bridge, not pausing or slowing as the light rain fell down on him.

–⩗–

Natalie was kneeling beside a dumpster, a block from the Burnside Bridge, near the railroad tracks. She wore blue coveralls, heavy leather boots. Tearing pages from the stash in her jacket's pockets, she twisted their edges and wedged them here and there. The exposed paper edges flashed the color of skin and hair, long, painted fingernails, beckoning smiles.

Natalie did not feel the coolness of the summer rain. At the sound of Leon's footsteps, she turned her head and looked up, unsurprised.

"What are you doing?" he said.

"I don't know," she said. "Something—"

She held out an almost full page from a magazine at arm's length so both she and Leon could look at it. In the photograph, a naked woman stood next to a stained-glass window with her head thrown back, her arms over her head and tangled in a sheer white nightgown she was taking off—it was as if she were wrestling a ghost, and the smooth front of her body was pushed out, strong and rounded. The heavy breasts with their pale nipples, the sharp line below her navel, parallel to the floor, that was the tan line where her bikini had been and now was not— and all the white skin below the line, soft and inviting, stretching down to the soft V between her legs.

"So?" Leon said.

"This is Daina House," Natalie said. "The January Playmate, in the very first days of the Bicentennial. In her spare time, she loves working in her parents' backgammon company, to escape the crazy world of modeling."

She looked at the photograph one more time, then crumpled it up and rolled it under the dumpster.

"If you like her so much," Leon said, "why not keep her?"

"Because that's selfish," Natalie said. "I want to share her; she wants to be shared. I like to think of a person, finding her here—"

"I still don't get it," Leon said.

"Just the way they'll feel."

"So?" he said.

Natalie stood up, taller than him. The rain beaded up on her light brown hair, which folded thickly on her shoulders. It looked real, if somewhat crooked on her head. She touched Leon's arm and they began to walk, shoulder to shoulder, down the railroad tracks, on the wet and greasy wooden ties.

"Don't be impatient with me," she said.

"I'm afraid," he said.

"Don't be."

"That's not how it is, I can't just not be."

"Just walk here with me. Lean against me."

"Sometimes I don't know what I've been doing."

"Like you forget?" Natalie said, "Or you just lose time, skip over it?"

"Right."

"That's normal. It happens to everyone."

"Not in the same way," he said.

Trucks slid across the Morrison Bridge, ahead, their headlights dim. The sun was about to rise.

"What about the wire?" he said. "I miss it. Can we go?"

"No one calls," she said. "The locks are all changed. That's all over, I think, and I can't keep track—there's other places, I know. Switching stations—one pole I found where the arrestor's broken, where I can feel the surges humming three blocks away. Let's go there. Or another place; I know some things, what you need."

Leon looked down at his damp shoes, stretching to reach the next railroad tie with each step. He looked up and saw Kayla, standing in an alleyway; thirty feet away, in the rain, holding her skateboard. Her face pointed at him, with no expression. Slowly, he raised his hand, and waved, but Kayla did not wave back. Instead, she turned, set down her board, and pushed off, away.

"Now what," Natalie was saying, "were we talking about?"

"I know a place to go," Leon said. "I could take you places with wires—"

"That's it," she said. "You lose time, you skip over it, you forget. I almost forgot that we were talking about forgetting. And forgetting—that happens to everyone. That's not the problem; we just have to let ourselves forget. We can't stay in the same place doing the same thing over and over and over again, reminding ourselves, keeping track."

"That's what I'm saying," Leon said. "That's what I'm doing."

"You can't worry about forgetting," she said. "It's a matter of blending in, and attractive clothing. Listen to me. We'll move forward."

"What?" he said. "My parents."

"What about them?"

"They took me to the hospital. Two days, two nights. Looking at pictures, doing puzzles. They put me in machines and looked at my skeleton, and my heart, and my brain—"

"And?"

"And all they want is to ask me questions—"

"Oh," Natalie said, "that's exactly how it is, once questions start you're only looking backward. You're right— we're the same, that way, we can't like questions. You have to get away from them; you can't let them slow you, make you doubt."

Cars honked at each other on the distant bridges; pale wet headlights slid along.

"I'm afraid."

"Don't be."

"That's not how it is, I just can't not be."

"I know some things," she said. "What you need."

"And they don't even know if there's anything different about me—they're going to test me more, I think, keep me in the hospital for a really long time."

"It's that no one calls," she said. "That makes me anxious. All the locks have been changed. My keys don't fit."

"I just don't know the answers," he said. "And the thing is, I don't feel bad."

"Of course you don't," she said. "Only different. And they'll never understand, but they'll try to slow you down. They'll come with question after question."

Natalie stopped walking, and so did Leon. She untwisted a piece of copper wire from around her neck and put it around his. Tight, it pressed a line in the skin of his throat.

22.

THE FISH IN THE TANK swam yellow and black, gold and white, with scales like armor. Koi. Some were as long as Chris's leg. Kayla reached out, her fingers breaking the water's surface—fish slid closer, believing it was feeding time—and the Asian woman behind the store's counter suddenly hissed:

"Boys! Step back, you two. No touching."

"I'm a girl," Kayla said.

The woman didn't answer. She returned to sorting receipts, and Chris and Kayla talked softly, watching the fish, not looking at each other.

"His parents called mine again," Chris said. "I haven't even seen him for a week."

"I saw him a couple mornings ago, at the skatepark. But what we're going to do today is for Leon, to help him, so we can understand what's going on."

"And what are we going to do?"

"You'll see." Kayla looked over at the woman again, raising her voice. "How much for the big ones?"

"Too much for you. They're twenty years old."

"So?"

"More than a thousand," the woman said.

"The little ones will live longer," Kayla said. "That doesn't make sense."

"Not too many get that big."

Outside, it was growing dark. Kayla looked back at Chris, then pointed to the white face of a clock on the wall.

The air outside wasn't any fresher; there was no wind at all. Across the street stood the store they were watching, Shanghai Shanghai, the gold words painted directly on the window. Kayla led Chris across to it; they stood two doors down, waiting. Nearby, the tall red gate spanned the street, covered in gold symbols even Kayla couldn't read. The gate rested on marble, and on gold lions, their bodies big as cars, kneeling there with pathetic expressions on their faces. Homeless people leaned against the lions, panhandlers drifted up from the Rescue Mission and the soup kitchens. Chris and Kayla paid no attention; they watched Shanghai Shanghai.

And then fingers grasped the bottom of the OPEN sign in the window, spun it to CLOSED. The man emerged all at once, his bald black head glinting before he put on a hat with a gold band, a turned up brim. He walked past them, and his gaze was high above them, looking beyond where anyone else could see. As he walked away in his pleated suit, copper bracelets flashed at his wrists, faintly clattered together. The people on the sidewalk parted as he approached them, giving him plenty of room. He turned the corner and was gone.

"He won't be back," Kayla said.

"What?"

"I watched him last night and the one before." She looked up and down the street. "We could pick the lock, but someone would see. Come on. Follow me."

They gave no one spare change as they walked, searching. They tried two wrong alleys before they found the right one. The green dumpster had been moved, which made it all more difficult to recognize, and the cover was on the manhole, slowing them. Kayla pried it open using the skate tool in her pocket, but it still took ten minutes, with both she and Chris sweating, anxiously checking the street behind them. When the cover slid away, they both stepped back, as if something or someone was awaiting them, ready to emerge from below. Cool, damp air rose.

Kayla turned and went down first, her shaved head disappearing, and Chris followed.

Together in the tunnel, the round circle of light slipping away, above and behind them, they held hands, and still bumped into each other. They could hear each other's breathing. They whispered.

"Did you hear someone?"

"I don't know."

"Shadows."

"I know."

They passed makeshift, underground storerooms, huge cans of peanut oil and bags of rice on shelves. Overhead, pipes snaked in every direction, circled by the shining rings of stainless steel clamps.

And then there were voices, and lights—flashlights, tight beams, round and bright. A group of people approached; Kayla and Chris hid along the shadowed wall, out of sight.

One man wore a headlamp and walked out in front, talking. The lamp illuminated his long, frizzy hair; when he turned, it shone on the faces of the people—four other adults, two children—who were listening.

"While sailors were shanghaied in other cities," he was saying, "Portland is unique because it's believed that men were actually kept here for periods of time, a ready supply of sailors." He turned his head, shining the light on a window cut in the wall, metal bars across it. "These tunnels run all the way from Twenty-third to the Willamette River, so you can imagine the extent of the labyrinth."

One of the children interrupted him, asking something.

"Are the tunnels haunted?" the guide said. "No, of course not—though people make up all kinds of stories."

"Why didn't they run away?" a woman asked.

"Well, they were locked in, and sometimes drugged, and you've probably noticed how the floor of the tunnels is covered in broken glass—those who were caught had to take off their shoes and go barefoot. I'll show you the pile of old boots, a little later."

Chris thought he heard footsteps, saw a movement in the darkness, in the other direction, a person hunching along. Chris pointed, trying to direct Kayla's attention, but she could not see his hand. Now, the group was almost past them, clustered together. Kayla pulled Chris along, sideways, as the guide led the people away.

The two of them moved slowly, by touch, finding the tight, hidden openings that were not doors, only broken-out bricks. The tunnel seemed to end, then turned back upon itself, blindly, all rough concrete and broken edges, and seemed to end again. They remembered this section, from the time before; they knew they were headed in the right direction. The air around them hung heavy and still, greasy, even hotter as they entered another passageway.

A thin shaft of light filtered down through a loose floorboard overhead, and in it they saw the flash of a face, twenty feet away. It was the bearded man, the man they'd seen before. He moved carefully, yet confidently; he did not need a flashlight here.

"Victor," Kayla said, under her breath. "Victor Machado."

"What?"

"Shh."

Carefully, they followed the man, crouching silently as he stepped into a nook in the wall, into a space the size of a closet. He loosened his clothes, then began pulling at the walls; he seemed to hold snakes—they were conduits, cables, wires. He began to wrap them around himself.

Chris stifled a sneeze, dirt in his nose, cobwebs on his face and in his hair. He leaned closer, trying to see, but Kayla held him back, in the blackest shadows. She pulled him away, down the tunnel, and finally stopped at another tight space like the one the man had gone into. They both stepped inside.

"This is an electrical vault," she said, whispering. "I read about them. All this; you see, these are phone lines— we could even tap Chesterton's line, if we got another headset—"

"Who?"

"And there are special phone lines for the police, somewhere, too, but mostly it's all electrical, high voltage stepped down for buildings. This round thing's a transformer, same as up on a pole."

"What was he doing back there?" Chris said. "That guy?"

"Quiet," she said.

As they stepped out of the vault, into the tunnel, they heard something, and then the shadows shifted as someone approached. It was a woman, slipping from darkness to darkness, with short, black hair, an unfamiliar face. Oblivious, she didn't see them, but moved past, into the vault, and began arranging the wires.

"Let's go," Kayla whispered. "We're wasting time. We're almost there." She pointed ahead, at the pale square of plywood that covered the entrance to the store. Before they reached it, though, they passed a third electrical vault.

Leon stood there, looking out, as if waiting to join them, to say something. But he did not. His body trembled; it did not move. His arms were hooked into cables, supporting his weight, and two wires were bent so one pressed against his forehead, one at the back of his head, holding it steady, looking out at them. Only he didn't see them through his wide eyes, his jerking eyelids; the skin of his cheeks was stretched tight and shifting in waves, a current running through it. His lips were pulled back, his teeth clenched. His shirt was torn at the neck, his pants unbuttoned, his shoelaces snaking loose and white along the dark ground.

"We have to get him out." Chris touched Leon's arm and it shocked him, jerked his hand back at him.

"No," Kayla said. "Don't touch him. He's fine—believe me, he's fine. I know. This is just what Victor was starting to do, back there. He was tapping in."

"How do you know that? How do you know the names?"

"Come on," she said, impatient.

"If this is what we're going to do," Chris said. "I don't know if I want to."

"This isn't for us," she said. "We're not like they are."

She took his hand and pulled him away from Leon, toward the plywood and the tight tunnel hidden behind it.

Kayla went in first and he crawled as fast as he could,

trying to keep up. He had splinters in his hands. The trap-door opened ahead—he heard it, saw the light, felt the change in pressure—and then he was pulling himself up into the store. The glass bottles on the shelves rattled, still settling from the trapdoor's slap.

"Hurry, Chris."

"This isn't helping me understand."

They whispered, though they were alone. Kayla was closing the trapdoor, pulling the threadbare rug back across it. The sparse merchandise around them cut strange silhouettes, a metal wind chime hung silent, the copper displays glinted, dull, and the unreadable calendars glowed white on the wall, covered in black symbols.

They hurried up the stairs. Glass from the tunnels was stuck in the rubber soles of their shoes, and it tapped on the floor as they climbed, as they raced down the hallway. A light shone in the first room they passed, empty, its walls covered in maps. Kayla opened the second door, where they'd stopped and listened, the last time.

Inside, the room looked kind of like a laboratory. All white, with metal counters and cabinets, two bare cots set out in the middle.

"What if I leave now?" Chris said.

"Take off your clothes," Kayla said. She was hurrying around the room, opening cabinets and drawers as if she knew what she was looking for. "You remember; you heard him. It works better that way."

She had wires in one hand and shucked down her

pants with the other. Chris stood in the middle of the room, watching her; he took off his shirt, folded it, unfolded it, and folded it again. Kayla wore only her bra now and held out two flat pieces of copper-colored metal, held together by wires.

"These go on your chest and back. Here."

The metal was cold; he hunched away from the plates on his chest, and that forced his spine into the one on his back. He shivered. Wires trailed, snarled, their ends dragging along the ground, shedding copper splinters.

"This looks like the same wire we used to get for Natalie," he said.

"Lay down on that cot," Kayla said.

He did, and she kept moving around him, making preparations. She fit a kind of necklace onto him, an armband. She twisted wires together. She hooked the loose ends of those trailing from him into the holes in the copper plates she wore. She fit the loose ends of her own wires into holes in his plates.

"Stop moving," she said, attaching a frayed end to the piece around his waist. Her hand was inches from his dick, which stirred, half-hard, pointing at her, but she didn't notice, didn't say a thing.

He closed his eyes and heard her step back, heard her cot shift beneath her, and then there was only her breathing, just beyond his, and outside a car horn, a shout, the roar of distant traffic, and her breathing, and his own, slow, pulling him inside. The dimness, the inside of his eyelids peeled away like black clouds he was passing through, and it was as if he were high above the trees, all their leaves, swooping lower toward a round pond that was not a pond, though it was full of water—

"What?" Kayla said. "What are you saying? You're mumbling too much."

"I can see us," he said. "Up on top of the tank in Forest Park. You're pretending to swim, throwing your white shirt off the edge and I can see it floating down into the tall grass. Now we're sitting on the foam rubber, in our underwear, and the sun is bright and we're looking at each other—"

Chris opened his eyes. Kayla was watching him, stretched out naked on the cot next to him, naked except for the copper pieces held on by wires; more wires stretched across the gap between the cots, to him. Her face looked like she was in pain, inside somewhere, like she was ignoring it, trying not to let him see.

"Go ahead," she said. "Close your eyes. Keep talking. Keep telling me."

He closed his eyes and saw the gray of the concrete, the red and blue of spray paint.

"It's under Burnside," he said. "The skatepark. It's you, Kayla, only you're not skating. You're sitting there, and putting on makeup. You're sitting on your skateboard, and you're reading—I can see you writing in a notebook, and there's another notebook inside it, and now you open it— you're checking to make sure no one can see, but I can see, and the handwriting inside this notebook is not your handwriting, and there's drawings, of two bodies, like diagrams with lines between them that are wires, that are marked down as wires—"

"Wake up!" Kayla was saying. "Chris! Wake up! We should go, get out of here."

He opened his eyes and could not see the skatepark. He was in the white room, and Kayla was jerking the wires from him, untwisting them.

"Just like I thought," Kayla said.

"What?" he said.

"Later," she said, panting, half-dressed, leaning close to untwist wires from his neck, his waist.

He crawled around, finding his clothes, which had been kicked to the walls. His hands shook as he pulled on his pants, tried to lace his shoes.

"Hurry," Kayla said.

They ran like someone was after them, like there was no more time, down the hallway, the stairs—Chris almost falling, his shirt over his head, pulled on just as they reached the bottom, where Kayla started lifting the trapdoor.

"Can't we go out the front?" he said.

"No, no," she said, holding it open for him, following him under, through the dark, tight tunnel, past the plywood, into the damp, wide tunnel with its sour air, its buzz of electricity.

Chris was out in front, but still catching up with his mind, rushing through the darkness. He had the same feeling as when the trucks on his skateboard began to wobble, when he was skating down a steep hill and there was no way to regain steadiness, at that speed, to avoid the crash, only the inescapable knowledge that it was coming. And his joints were sore, too, like after skating, wiping out, surprising hitches in his knees and elbows as he moved through the darkness.

The electrical vault where Leon had been was empty, but the woman was in the next one—wrapped in wires, her shirt unbuttoned, her head steadied, her eyes rolled back, white. She trembled. She could not see them.

"Who is she?"

"That doesn't matter."

The last vault was also empty. Kayla and Chris stood still for a moment. There were no lights, no voices, no motions in the shadows. Holding hands, they rushed back through the labyrinth, shards of glass crushed to powder beneath their feet. They pushed and pulled each other all the way back to the ladder.

Squinting, they emerged into the alley. They did not speak, did not look at each other. With their feet, they kicked, they slid the heavy cover back over the manhole, and then they walked out into the sidewalk, into the stream of pedestrians, under the streetlights.

They walked two blocks, past Hung Far Low restaurant, past whole blocks of parking lots. Down past Flanders Street, a dog in a parked car suddenly lunged barking through a half-open window, and Chris veered into Kayla.

They both stopped walking, realizing they could. They looked at each other, not certain how to begin.

"Pretty weird," she said. "Don't you think?"

"I don't know," Chris said. "Did that happen? What was that notebook?"

"A notebook I found, that's all." Dirt and copper splinters showed in the stubble of Kayla's hair, against her scalp.

"You haven't been telling me," Chris said.

"You'll know everything I do," she said, "really soon— I mean, it's better, you're better for it than I am, since I already have some guesses that might be wrong, or get in my way—"

"We're not supposed to have secrets," he said. "That's not right. That's how everything started going bad."

"That's not how," she said. "I'm going to tell you how, I'm going to show you so you'll understand."

"You should have already shown me."

"That's what I'm doing!" Kayla stepped closer; she reached out, touched the skin of Chris's arm. "One thing—we can't tell Leon that we saw him like that."

"Why not?"

"He won't understand."

"He definitely won't," Chris said, "if we don't tell him."

"Trust me," Kayla said. "Just for a little while. It's for Leon, the three of us."

23.

STEVEN OPENED HIS EYES onto Heather's broad, pale back, the knobs of her vertebrae, the line of dark moles along one shoulderblade, her brown hair spread across the pale flowers of the pillowcase. Beyond her, he could see the tall dresser of chipped blond veneer, the framed mirror that made him feel sad, just the sight of it, and the painting that showed a child being disciplined, sent to a corner, facing the wall. A collie stood next to the child, looking out with pained eyes, a sympathetic expression on its long, thin snout. In script below, the title read *The Silent Pleader*. Across the bedroom, the painting on the far wall was a hunting scene—a black Labrador in mid-air, leaping over tall grass with its tail a sharp sword behind it, its tongue and ears flapping, a V of geese or ducks overhead. Steven wondered if Heather had chosen these paintings of dogs, and when, or if it had been someone else, more recently, either describing them to her or deciding what she would desire.

The cat came into the bedroom, walked across the floor, and leapt onto the windowsill. Outside, it was raining, gray; the clouds, the rain filtered the light. Steven wanted to check his watch, but it was on the bedside table, face down, and he didn't want to wake Heather by reaching across her. Instead, he leaned closer, felt the warmth of her body against his face, smelled her skin.

"Let's talk about what we did in Chinatown," she said.

"I thought you were asleep."

"I was thinking. Why haven't we talked about it? It's been days."

"We agreed not to," he said.

"I thought it would be better if you brought it up, to see how long you waited." Heather turned over, so their faces were close together, her eyes closed.

"You could have said something," he said. "I did want to talk about it, and I didn't."

"I am," she said. "I mean, what happened is only between the two of us, and who would believe it, if we tried to tell someone else? It'd be kind of hard to explain."

"I was just a guest," he said. "You were the one that guy invited."

"Chesterton." Heather rolled her neck, stretching, her face flashing at the ceiling, her head moving across the pillowcase, exposing a faded flower. Reaching out, she slapped the box on the bedside table, and a remote, mechanical voice said "Seven-thirty-seven A.M."

"An hour and a half until we have to be at The Seeing

Eye," she said. "Stay in bed. Stay right here."

"I don't like to eat in bed," he said, "if that's what you're thinking. The crumbs."

"I want to talk," she said. "I want to talk about what I saw."

"All right," he said. "Let's talk."

"The thing is, I saw it all—the colors, the woman undressing. I could really *see* it. I've been thinking and thinking about it. Once, I read somewhere that if you were born blind, or went blind, even, that those parts of your brain shut down, those visual parts. But in that room I could see, even if what I saw happened some other time."

Steven tried to move closer to Heather, to touch the length of his body to hers; his shifting felt obvious, strained. He stopped, inches from her. A bus splashed past, outside, and someone's voice shouted in the rain. The cat leapt down from the windowsill, slid out into the hallway.

"I was wondering if my cat misses the river," Steven said.

"Are you trying to change the subject?" Heather pulled herself up, leaning against the headboard. The blanket slipped down over the two sharp bones of her clavicles, the tops of her breasts, her small, dark nipples.

"I did—I do want to talk about it," Steven said. "It was crazy, confusing—but I was embarrassed, too. I am." He paused, then continued with what he had to say. "What you were describing that day," he said. "That man you saw, that was me."

"I thought so," she said. "And that woman—she's someone you know?"

Her tone was even, impossible to read; with the guide dogs, too much mood in a voice, too much variation, brought confusion.

"Someone I knew," he said. "It was a just a mistake, a misunderstanding. This was before you and I were involved, before—"

"Why are you so nervous?" Heather said. "I'm just trying to understand what happened. No reason to be so defensive."

"Nothing happened," he said.

"I mean what happened when I saw it, when we were in the room with the wires."

"Did you really know it was me?"

"That made the most sense."

"Why?"

"Chesterton told me to bring someone—another blind person—who was someone I wanted to learn more about. That's why. Someone who might be keeping a secret from me."

"It's not like that," Steven said.

"Maybe not," she said. "But still, you were embarrassed, like you said—you didn't bring it up."

"I guess not."

"Why didn't you sleep with her?"

"Pardon me?"

"In that bedroom where I saw you, the woman was

undressing on the bed, posing for you—it was like she was waiting, inviting you to join her."

"Not exactly."

"Come on, Steven. That was obvious."

"I was afraid."

Heather smiled, squeezed his leg under the sheets. "You're not afraid of sex. I know that."

"I'm just embarrassed," he said. "I don't think it has to affect anything—"

"I saw you."

"She wasn't right," he said. "This person I knew. It was like she was acting, or something, and I couldn't understand why. She was like a different person, like it was some joke on me that I couldn't follow."

Steven ran his finger down Heather's arm, down along her ribs. She shivered. For a moment, he thought she was going to reach out for him.

"Nothing happened," he said.

"Well," Heather said. "You didn't have sex. But something *did* happen, and the main thing is that I saw it, whatever it was."

Now she did touch his forehead, his face. He turned his head, looking at the window. Three crows were perched outside, on a shaking electrical line; they stretched their necks, re-folded their black wings, and suddenly rose, clapping airborne just as a squirrel, tail aloft, came running down the wire.

"I don't know," he said. "It's all so strange—for instance,

what does this guy Chesterton get out of it?"

"I've wondered about that," Heather said. "And I can't tell. I think maybe he doesn't really know, either, like he's trying to figure out what he has. Or maybe he's just some kind of pervert, just wants to see people take their clothes off—"

Steven laughed. "And wire them together? But something happened. It's not that simple. I mean, you *saw*."

"I wonder if we'll get the chance to do it again," she said.

"Did he say so?"

"He has to call."

"We could just ask him. Find him."

"I don't think so," she said. "He seemed pretty strict about all that."

Heather lay with the crook of her elbow over her eyes, as if keeping out light. In the silence, Steven heard the cat jumping off something, running up and down the hardwood floor of the hallway.

"I want to tell you something," Heather said. "Don't laugh."

"All right."

"I want to see myself," she said.

"See yourself?"

"I can hardly remember what I look like," she said. "I mean, there are photographs that I can remember pretty exactly, but I was younger, then."

"I can tell you what you look like," Steven said.

"That's not the same," she said. "That's not what I'm talking about. I think maybe Chesterton could help, if we could do it again."

"What?"

"One person sees a secret the other one has," she said, "something they're keeping from someone. So I'm thinking that if we—you and I—do something together, some kind of secret thing, that I might be able to see myself, the way I look now."

"Maybe," he said. "I think I get what you're saying."

"So you'll help me?"

"I'll try."

Heather reached out and slapped the clock again; its alert voice said "Eight-twelve A.M." She threw the blankets aside and stood up. The day had begun.

24.

VII. CONTINUED REFLECTIONS

In the Affected, self-medication takes many forms. Electricity draws these individuals. One common source, in my experience, is the electrical vaults in the tunnels beneath the city. Here, the Affected expose high-voltage wires and press themselves against these wires; the individuals remain in this state, unresponsive for a period of time, and, once the requisite level of electricity is absorbed, they are set free.

Some of this is conjecture, of course; I must not assume that my limited knowledge is exhaustive, and I certainly cannot report what I have not seen—yet I have repeatedly observed the Affected as they rest suspended, underground. Here, their outward aspect (the twitching of their faces, and talking to people who are not present, their unawareness of people who are present) is strikingly similar to that of the UnAffected I have exposed to my process, upstairs, the indi-

viduals in my experiments. The question becomes how similar the interior experience of these two groups of individuals
might be...

...it's possible that the Affected may communicate with
others who are nearby, connected through the live electrical
lines, that they may share dreams or memories or interact in
ways that are not easy for us to grasp. Might they recognize
each other, after such interactions? Is their conscious life as
barren as it appears to be, or a shell hiding pleasures of grand
complexity? One of my frustrations...

...I do not wish to live forever; I do not want to die
before I find out what I need to know. I admit there are times
when I let my conjectures loose, when I hatch new possibilities in an attempt not to limit myself. I admit, for instance,
that I have half-believed, at times, that what I have uncovered, what I am witnessing is a glimpse into the world of the
dead. The Affected, after all, show no signs of aging. Admit-
tedly, I have lost track of some individuals (I've also wondered if they might disappear suddenly, gone with a whispering snap in a moment when they are unobserved), but
those I have tracked for years seem the same as on my first
appraisal...

...Yesterday, in a sort of desperation, I convinced Victor
to join me in an experiment. Upstairs, unclothed, I attached
the copper breastplates, the wires, and connected the two of

us. Had Victor not undone the wires, merely minutes later, I don't know what would have happened.

I remember nothing, only the feeling of a sharp heat, a soldering iron at my brain-stem, every muscle gone rigid. And then I opened my eyes and Victor was loose from me, nervous, muttering politely, as ever. A sweat shone on him an oxidizing perspiration that ran green across the copper plates, but he seemed otherwise unharmed. More alert, if anything. Sharper. He took off his chestplate, he scratched at the black hair it had covered, hair that matched his beard. I was still on the floor, my eyes even with his feet, the sharp bristles atop his toes. I could not rise. That one minute, being connected to an Affected individual, had completely drained me. I nearly had to go to the hospital. I scarcely made it off the floor, then slept for five days. I could not eat solid food for a week. It was as if all electricity had been leached from my body, each synapse gone dark.

This was perhaps an experiment that had to be attempted, but it is also one that will not be repeated...

Kayla wore a torn gray sweatshirt, a knit cap with orange and black stripes. The air held a damp chill; it was almost five in the morning, and she was skating—not under the bridge, but half a mile away, in the parking garage of the Radisson Hotel. She skated the circular ramp from top to bottom, corkscrewing, descending through the levels, and then she slowly climbed the concrete stairs to do it again.

As she climbed, she held her skateboard in one hand, Chesterton's open notebook in the other. The safety lights flickered above, just bright enough that she could read, that she could find her way through the passages she'd read so many times before. She'd reached the end, dissatisfied; yet as frustrating as she found the notebook, she doubted anyone could understand it any better. She had tried with Chris—read with him, explained the technical sections—and was not certain how far he followed, how much he grasped. All his attitude about secrets and honesty—he had to see past that, to realize how far beyond them Leon was, now.

Her board rang along the metal railing as she climbed, reading. The numbers, letters and colors—3B, Orange Level 4—passed in her peripheral vision, with glances of the few cars left overnight, their dark shapes and sharp angles casting shadows.

...The minds of the Affected, I've conjectured, are capable of flights we cannot imagine, experiences both complex and displaced. It is quite possible that these experiences are contiguous with the lives they lead here, and equally possible that there is no connection at all. Perhaps their displaced actions are all in my mind, or as mundane and boring as their lives here, and there is no sense of cause and effect, no increased illumination. I'm not even certain what I'm writing of, here...

...to articulate my dream—the beginning is merely to find a way to truly talk to the Affected, to earn their trust, to see if my simulations reflect in any way their experience, to find out what we might learn from them. Of course, here I am assuming a connection, a basis for communication, a commonality. I must admit that I have let myself be led by intuition, by hope, and that nothing I have found quite validates my desires. It only exasperates them.

At best, my experiments have found a conduit, a means by which secrets are unlocked, a vision into a guilty corner of another's mind. Is that all? And what memories do I retain, do I myself keep from the world? Nothing sufficiently interesting, nothing that might cast light? Things I have forgotten, repressed somehow? And how would these fragments of the past constitute a future? Here I am, seeking answers, beset by questions...

...How pathetic I sound, even to myself! I suppose that I want to be like the Affected, and not like them. I want to have it both ways, to experience what they experience and yet retain the insight, the ability to reflect upon it that they lack. I suspect this is impossible, that one is Affected or not Affected, and perhaps I lack the certainty, the knowledge or courage to pass to the other side...

Kayla reached the rooftop, stepping out of the stairwell, the cool gray sky overhead, the parking spots marked out in yellow lines beneath her feet. She clapped the notebook shut. Pathetic was right. Zipping the book into her backpack, she looked around herself, at the darkness easing from the sky. The parking attendants showed up at five-thirty, which was soon. Kneeling, she tightened her laces and felt the cool air on her elbows as they pushed out the holes in her sweatshirt. She tore loose threads from the fraying cuffs of her Dickies, then pulled on her worn leather gloves.

She pushed off, slow at first, over the yellow line, the word STOP, rolling along, following the curved concrete wall that was striped with the black lines of bumpers, tires, all aiming, pointing downward, around and around—she leaned in, hard, trying to stay in the tight curve, her balance pulling her out toward the edge, back into the middle as she funneled through—

—faster and faster, she wobbled and straightened in the funnel, shooting loose out into the fourth level, the long slants of concrete, the slalom through the pillars, the rail slide along the curb at the elevators, the slap of her palm on the red metal doors as she rolled by—she kicked twice for more speed as she passed single cars parked alone and lonely with black shadows beneath them, dark spaces behind the windows where someone could be sleeping—

—She listened for the jingle of key rings, the hinge of car doors opening, the bells of the elevators. Nothing, only the low echo of her own wheels as she dropped again into the tight spiral, down, down, down. Bending low to make the corners, her front hand out flat, less than an inch above the concrete—

—and then the long square of light, the street, the Stop signs. She leaned back, planted one gloved hand, and slid her board sideways, wheels screeching, her feet still on the board. She slid twenty feet, stretched out, her back parallel to the ground, her pack softly whispering against concrete. And then she was still, motionless, stopped next to the line of long metal teeth set into the ground, that kept cars from entering the wrong way.

Standing, she shivered and clapped her gloved hands together, keeping an eye on the glass booths—still empty, but she didn't have time to risk another run. The skating had been enough, though; it had focused her, helped her to filter Chesterton's sloppy thinking. As she'd expected, he could only take it so far—she could see where he was going more clearly than he could, to the obvious conclusions, the ones he didn't dare. He was an adult, after all. She could see where she herself was going, a place she couldn't afford, couldn't stand to be alone. She would find Chris, and together they would get straight with Leon.

Certainty coiled up inside Kayla, the clarity radiating outward. She smiled to herself, and stepped up on the metal teeth, balancing, bouncing, trying to get them to fold down. The teeth could tear tires to shreds, stop cars cold, and yet they couldn't harm her.

THREE

25.

HE HEARS THE MAN'S VOICE, then the sound of the gas cap unscrewed and slapped down, the metal of the nozzle fitting inside, the roar of the gasoline that speaks low to him, close to his ear. Who is he? Doesn't he like the way he's going? Is it today, again? He can smell the gasoline, too; he likes it. Now he hears Natalie's voice. This is her truck, where he lies hidden, flat in the covered bed. He is hidden under clothing, and his skateboard, all the old magazines and the wigs, their hair that smells like someone's head mixed with old perfume. He is under the scarves and stockings, all the sheer material, the shoes with sharp heels and thin straps. Under the new clothes she's bought him, the pleated pants and the plaid shirts—every time he wears a new one, he has to pull out the straight, sharp pins, take out the tissue paper folded inside. She says they are attractive clothes, the kind anyone would wear.

The truck is moving; he hears the highway and he

shifts his body a little, magazine pages slip over each other, showing all their words and skin. He waits. After a while or a long time, the truck stops, the engine still going, and he hears the door open, sees Natalie's head in the side window, walking around. She jerks the back open and the bright sun shines around her so he can't see her face, can't see her mouth when she speaks.

"Great work," she says. "You can ride up front, now."

She takes off her long, black hair; her head is bristly and round, like his. He feels her head, then his. She feels his, then her own. They are the same. At least twenty strands of copper wire rest tangled along the floor and seat between them, sharp ends pointing loose. At the other end, all the wires have been twisted and braided together, into a plug that fits tight in the round circle where the cigarette lighter had been. He picks up a loose wire and attaches it to his necklace, the copper wire around his neck. He twists another around each wrist—Natalie is doing the same, her eyes on the road—and his ankles, just above his new black boots that have no laces, just elastic at the ankles. A gentle, reassuring current flows. More might be better; this is barely enough.

"Holy crow!" Natalie says.

"Holy crow," he says.

"It's good to be moving," she says. "We have our own way of doing things."

"We'll see about that," he says.

"It won't be that tricky to change the way you look, if

we have to. You look like someone's son—that's good."

"Right," he says.

"Did I say that?" she says. "I don't know. It'll be home school, anyway."

Sometimes a building looks like a house, or a barn, or a store. He used to know words in German. You have to keep it up, to be reminded so you know the same thing every day even if it's wrong, Natalie says. And then you can forget and then remember different things, until you forget those, so you never get stuck—Natalie says she's feeling better and better, that she knows how people think. The copper wires are like a web stretching to her from the dashboard. The wires go straight through her earlobes, where they are pierced, pulling slightly so her ears stick out; other wires disappear inside her shirt, between the buttons, attached to something inside. She is smiling, talking, driving.

"It's a nice gesture," she says, "but I have plenty of money for us."

Outside, it's flat desert, sagebrush, low trees he doesn't know the names of. Metal transformer towers run along each side of the road like friendly giants against the pale blue sky.

"I've had these boots a long time?" he says.

"Those clothes are attractive," she says, "the kind anyone would wear."

All the water had been on the right side, the ocean, and the tall pine trees. Spruce, juniper, pine. Natalie knows all the names. That was yesterday, or the day before, or today. The sun is jumping all over the sky, and sometimes it's the moon. He can still remember the names of his friends, but that's about all. He hopes they are doing all right, whatever they are doing. He remembers his family, a little. There were some of them, that he lived with. He does know Natalie, who is humming a song that is the static on the radio. She turns it up and he feels it in the wires, passing through him, up his legs and arms, around and around his neck as he turns it to look at her. They are driving straight down the middle of California. She shows him the map. He knows Natalie, though her name is now Susan. He feels himself forgetting and then remembering the name and losing it again.

"Friends?" she says. "I'll be your friend. I'll find you friends, if I'm not enough—I can do that."

"In our house," he says. "We're almost there."

They eat sour candy shaped like worms. Red and yellow and green. Bag after bag of them. The wires tremble as they chew. She is talking, and he knows she is speaking straight from her thoughts, without planning or hesitations, and that what she says is true, that she'll make it so, that he'll help her.

"For someone to follow, they'd need to be like us, to think that way, and if they were like us then they wouldn't want to follow."

"Is that a riddle?"

"Exactly," she says. "What were we talking about, again?"

"Trees?"

"Right. Well, there aren't any trees, here."

"What's my name, again?" he says.

"Paul," she says. "Isn't that what I said, before? Anyway—Paul."

"Paul," he says. Turning, he looks into the bed of the truck and sees the empty wigs trembling like small dogs. He sees all the clothes and magazines that someone could hide beneath.

"This is our truck." He looks at her and remembers the holes in his own ears; picking up a loose wire, he forces its sharp tip through, twists it on itself.

"Friends, friends," she says. "And what's my name?"

"Susan," he says.

"Good," she says. "Susan. And if I need you to call me something else, I'll tell you. We can practice."

The sun is bright on her face, shining along the wires. Her arms fit between the wires, her hands on the steering wheel, aiming the truck. The vehicles on every side are all colors and sizes. Some pass the truck, too fast; some, too slow, the truck passes. Vehicles drive on and off the highway.

"But I've hardly got any hair under my arms," he says. "Or between my legs."

"It's not so great as people say," she says.

Outside, some cows are standing in a corral. Some horses are standing in a corral. It's morning. It's afternoon.

"Is it high school I'm going to?"

"It'll be home school, anyway. I'll teach you."

"I'm not wearing wigs," he says.

"No one said you have to."

"I brought all the money. Where did I get it, again?"

"It's a nice gesture," she says, "but I have plenty of money for us. Yours won't be necessary. Save it."

Green fields surround them. Water shoots clear, then white, from irrigation lines. Distant hills are lined with rows of white windmills—tall and slender, their three-spoked heads spin in different directions, at different speeds. She sees them and points, and smiles.

"The windmills generate electricity," he says. "They store it up."

"We'll string wires straight from it," she says, "out in the yard, all through the rooms of our house. Always within arm's reach."

"In our house," he says. "We're almost there."

"We'll be friends; we'll have friends. We'll be good neighbors."

"We have our own ways of doing things," he says.

"We'll buy a house with a windmill," she says.

"Or we'll buy a house and build a windmill." He knows this part, recognizes it, believes it. "Or buy a wind-mill and build a house."

"We will," she says.

26.

A DINNER CRUISE drifted up the dark river, only the strings of lights along its decks revealing the size of the huge boat as it slipped past Oaks Park, past the dark Ferris wheel and the black bones of the rollercoaster. All the rides were silent; tonight was Wednesday, and the park was only open on weekends, this late in the season.

Chris and Kayla walked along the train tracks that ran past the back of the parking lot.

"I'm so glad," she said. "I can't hardly stand waiting anymore."

Chris was watching the amusement park, the bright point of the watchman's cigarette, near the bumper cars; then he looked away, to the left, across the shallow black water of the bird refuge, the broken-off trees, the jagged, drowned stumps. Up on the hill, the crematorium loomed, pale and square. The moon was a sliver, the sky dark; Chris wondered if they were burning the bodies now, when the smoke would blend into the sky. How long did it take to burn up a dead person? Did they burn faster, like dry wood?

"What?" Kayla said.

"I feel like we got older this summer," he said. "Like how we forgot how we started it, what we wanted to do. And now it's almost school again. At least then we'll see Leon—he'll have to come to school."

"You haven't heard from him, either?"

"His parents called, a couple nights ago, wondering where he was. They said to call if I saw him. I should have told them to call me, too. I should call—I will, later."

Electrical lines ran next to the tracks, the narrow towers running six wires—three on each side, hanging off insulators—that stretched straight from where they had been to where they were going.

"Don't worry so much," Kayla said. She kicked an empty glass bottle and it bounced along the rail, hollowly, not shattering. To the right, headlights shifted along the Sellwood Bridge. Houseboats, dark and quiet, rested in their harbors below.

"Is there ever a train on these tracks?" Chris said.

"Hardly ever," Kayla said.

They walked. Blackberry bushes clustered tight on each side of the tracks, their leafy surfaces shifting slightly, as if breathing, as if someone slept beneath their cover. Chris flinched as a cat slipped out, then hunched past, heading the other direction, ten feet away and not even paying attention.

"We have to think like Leon to really find him," Kayla was saying.

Chris looked over his shoulder; now that the cat was out of sight, he realized it had been a raccoon.

"Everything we need is in the notebooks," she said, "in my backpack—"

The tracks curved to the left, up a slight hill, away from the river, closer to the neighborhood, the dark silhouettes of houses.

"I knew a kid who lived up that street," Chris said, pointing. "They had a strobe light in their basement, and a ping-pong table."

Almost every window was dark, everyone inside asleep. As Chris and Kayla kept moving along the track, they left a sporadic trail of barking dogs behind them. Somewhere, down a side street, the tinny music of an ice cream truck sounded, out of place and time. They paused, then kept walking, around the back of a big, abandoned building. Chris had to hurry to keep up with her pace. And then the air tightened around them, a low hum when he listened close.

SELLWOOD SUBSTATIONS, the sign read, attached to a tall chain-link gate. DANGER, read another, showing a lightning bolt striking a stick man in the chest, knocking him backward.

"Here we are," Kayla said.

Vines climbed thick through the tall fence; squinting,

Chris saw inside, the cluster of tall transformers, the switching towers, all the lines coming and going. He flinched at a crackle overhead. The structures inside were bigger than houses, towers of girders connected like erector sets, shadowy, like the metal skeletons of buildings without walls, floors or ceilings. And all this vibrated in the half-light, the hum. Lanterns—attached down low, old fashioned, some not working—cast pale, overlapping circles along white gravel. The substation stretched; it took up the whole block. Wires snaked everywhere, in and out of transformer drums shaped like huge batteries, like rockets.

"I know," Kayla said, watching him take it all in.

"You've been here before?"

"A lot. Figuring it out, studying the voltage and everything."

A car drove past, headlights sweeping around them before bouncing high, the whole thing clattering over a speed bump, its red taillights fading.

"We have to go around here," Kayla said. "We're out in the open, right under this light where anyone can see us."

Chris followed her around the corner, onto Linn Street, and into the bushes. Here, an eight-foot concrete wall alternated with short stretches of chain-link. Kayla stopped at one of these stretches, crouching in the bushes' shadows. She set her pack on the ground, knelt, and unzipped it. Slowly, she pulled out a tangle of metal and wire, wrapped it in on itself, and heaved it over the fence.

It unsnarled through the air, into the lights, and kicked up gravel where it landed.

"What was that?"

"You afraid?" Kayla said.

"Yes," he said.

She stood, a wire-cutter in her hands. She climbed up the fence, cut the three strands of barbed wire at the top, then jumped back down. Another dog started barking; Chris wondered if it was barking at them or someone else.

Kayla went over, and he followed, landing next to her, inside. The dog had stopped barking. Was the air even tighter, heavier, more charged inside the fence? It felt that way. Chris shivered, the gravel sharp beneath his feet. Was anyone watching? Were there alarms? He wanted to believe; he still trusted Kayla. She picked up the wires she'd thrown over and kept walking, untangling them; her hair was soft looking again, the bristles grown long enough to mostly lie flat. The lights shone eerily, making the white gravel glow, exposing them as if they were on a stage, surrounded by the whole dark neighborhood. They hurried under the switching towers, the transformers, their pale shadows cast by the lamplight in every direction, dark spokes shifting gently around them.

Chris listened to the fans, the crackle in the air, just beneath the surface, and to Kayla as she explained it all— pointing out the transformers, the incoming transmission lines, high-voltage, and the smaller lines going out.

"Seventy-two hundred volts," she said. "Household voltage."

"What are we doing?"

"We're climbing. No, not that side. You want to kill us? This one here is us. I've figured it all out. How much do you weigh, anyway?"

"One-twenty," Chris said.

"Good," she said. "Here, climb up here. Stand on that platform. Don't touch anything, yet. And listen to me, that's the main thing. We have to keep talking to each other."

"What?"

"It'll get bad," she said, standing beneath him. "It has to, if we do it right, so just hold on and try to talk as long as you can."

The metal of the girders was like a ladder, easy to climb. He could feel Kayla, now, climbing beneath him, and he moved squinting past the lantern, to a narrow platform about fifteen feet above the ground. A row of some kind of transformers stood there, white like four-foot-tall sparkplugs, wires stretching from their tops. Below, the whiteness spread in every direction; above, the dark, the shadowy wires.

Now Kayla was next to him, leaning close, her shoulder touching his. She put something in his hand, a metal piece that was the handle of a hacksaw, perhaps, connected by thick strands of copper wire to another handle, one she held.

"We each hold these and then—when I say 'three,' take hold of that wire with your outside hand. There, just above the transformer."

"Why don't we do it one at a time?" he said. "Would that be safer?"

"This is the way I figured it out," she said. "We just have to keep talking. If I don't answer, you break the connection. Same with me. That way we'll be all right."

Chris stood, looking at her in the half-light. He felt the metal grid sharp beneath his bare feet, through his shoes.

"One, two, three," she said.

They each grasped the thick wire above the transformers. At first, it was like nothing.

"How long?" Chris said.

"Ten minutes, maybe—I wanted it to be slow, safe."

"What?"

"As long as it takes."

At this height, the gravel looked smooth, one solid piece, soft and milky, like he could fall into it and not be hurt. The sky overhead stretched blue-black, shot with stars. And Kayla's skin shone, so pale, tinged blue, almost, veins forking in her chest, up her throat, her head beginning to tremble, or maybe that was his own head, his vision shaky. He felt a pricking along the surface of his skin, sharp and then dissipating. Next, a hollow ache in his bones, and he could sense every piece of his skeleton, aware of the sharpness beneath his skin.

"Chris!" Kayla said. "Talk to me."

"It hurts," he said, his words coming out wobbly, his jaw's hinges tight. "I'm talking. I don't know what to say."

"Listen," she said. "You know what? Leon took all our money, up in Forest Park? I didn't tell you that yet."

"You went there alone?" he said. "Without me?"

"Just to check," she said, "but the bank was empty, and there was just a note from Leon, saying he needed the money, and good-bye."

"What?"

"But we'll find him," she said. "Don't worry. After this, we'll understand him."

Chris's eyes trembled and snapped, dry—was that the sound in his ears? He looked at Kayla, tried to, his vision unsteady and slipping past her. Did he see movement in the bushes, a figure standing at the fence they'd climbed?

"Chris!" she said.

"I'm here," he said. "Maybe we should stop?"

"Listen, here's a funny thing I was thinking—you know how when kids go missing they make those computer-aged pictures of them? Milk cartons or whatever? For Leon, you know, the face will change to look like someone he'll never be, older, and for us, maybe—"

"I see someone," he said.

"It's me," she said. "Just me. Hold on; don't get weird. We're close."

"No," he said. "Behind you. Someone's coming."

The figure was over the fence, now. He walked closer, shadows jerking out smoothly on every side, wearing shiny black shoes, creased pants and a white shirt, with Kayla's pack on his back. Standing below them, he tilted his head to look up, his serious face framed by his black beard.

"Victor!" Kayla shouted, her voice shaky and strange. "Put down my pack. Go back outside."

"I'm coming to help you," the man said. "I'm coming to play with you."

"That's the guy from the tunnel," Chris said. "You know him?"

"Just his name," she said. "Read about him." She shouted again: "Go away! Put down my pack!"

"I've been following you," the man said. "I saw you. I'm not supposed to, but then I thought I should, also. Because I wanted to." He began to climb the tower next to the one they were on. His long arms and legs stretched and bent sharply as he rose.

Chris could no longer feel the metal beneath his feet, anything at the edges of his body, his skin. He did feel Kayla, next to him, as close as if they were touching, both watching the man climb.

"Kayla," Chris said. "Kayla." His words were coming apart, her name. He tried to drop the metal handle and his fingers clenched tighter; he could not let go.

Now the man had reached the same level and stood on a platform fifteen feet away. Turning, he faced them and smiled.

"I followed you all the way," he was saying. "It's great; finally!" He kicked off his pointed black shoes and they bounced and settled against the white gravel below. He unbuttoned his white shirt, top to bottom, his chest all black hair. Smiling still, checking them, he reached out, for balance, his long arm stretching for a cable, and the current arced to him, even as he kept talking.

"We can do it! We can have a lot of fun together!"

The electricity snaked blue around his shoulder; Kayla's pack smoldered, then turned to flames, a round ball of fire on his back. In a moment, his beard was gone. His white face glowed as his body jerked, held there, sparks bouncing down through the grate, lost against the light and the white gravel. The electricity wrapped him head-first in a net of blue sparks that slowed into red flames. The flames twisted in on themselves, dark convulsions at their center, which was Victor. They pulled at him; his burning body fell.

Kayla looked away, up, and saw the surge flowing through the wires above them, all her calculations shot and tweaked; the charge floated blue along surfaces, inevitably closer, straight down on them, irresistible. She kicked Chris, kicked him away, his hands loose. His knees buckled, but he did not fall.

Chris turned, his skin numbed and hurting, ringing; he slapped at Kayla until the handles rang loose, swinging and sparking on the metal. Overhead, lazy electrical flickers bounced back and forth along the wires, slowing and sputtering as the arrestors kicked in, the safeguard switches, the cut-offs.

"Come on," Kayla said.

The two climbed down, trembling, feet numb on the sharp, white gravel. They walked slowly past the cinders of Kayla's pack, past Victor's black shoes.

Victor lay stretched flat on his back, motionless. His eyes stared straight up, his long thin arms straight out from his sides. His hair had all been singed away, his face gray and charred; his shirt had burned off, his black pants melted into the flesh of his legs.

"Is he dead?" Chris said.

"He wasn't exactly alive," Kayla said.

An alarm sounded, answered after a moment by distant sirens. Kayla pulled Chris away. They climbed the fence, shuffled along through the dark neighborhood. The streetlights overhead snuffed out one at a time, a darkness cast out in waves from the substation.

27.

STEVEN DROVE HIS CAR WEST, across the Burnside Bridge. He turned right on Fourth Avenue, under the tall red gate, and parked. Chinatown was relatively small, and the land-marks—the gate, the Cindy's Adult Book Store and Japanese Happy Fast Bowl signs—he'd sighted on that strange day were apparent. Finding the shop was easier than he'd anticipated.

He put two quarters in the parking meter and walked down the sidewalk, rubbing his hands together. At Shanghai Shanghai, he paused, then pushed the glass door open and stepped into the dim light.

Paper lanterns, hanging from the ceiling, shivered in the draft as the door closed behind him. The shelves seemed less dusty than he remembered, more full and organized, yet he knew immediately that this was the same place.

"May I help you, sir?" A middle-aged Asian man in a

white apron stood at the counter. He smiled, his black hair parted and shining, his hands clasped.

"Is he here, the owner?" Steven said.

"I am the owner. Henry Yee."

"Chesterton," Steven said. "I think he's the one. A tall black man?"

"Perhaps you could explain how I might help you."

"I appreciate that," Steven said. "But I really don't think you can help me."

The man held his hands above the counter, trying to appear patient.

"It's difficult to be certain of that," he said, "when what you desire is so unclear to me."

Steven stepped closer. Outside the front windows, cars jerked through potholes, conversations drifted closer and faded away.

"I know it's not something that's necessarily talked about," he said, "but do you know anything about the operation upstairs?"

"Upstairs?" The man looked toward the back of the shop, where the stairway stretched into darkness.

"I know about it," Steven said. "I've been there before."

"There's nothing upstairs."

"Do you mind if I go up there, just to see?"

"Suit yourself."

The lights on the stairs were out, but the hallway at the top shone, daylight coming through the windows. Steven hurried upward, pausing in the doorway of the first room—it was empty, swept clean, nothing left except the four round marks on the floor where a table had stood, cork walls stuck with blue-, red- and white-headed pins.

The second room—the one he had been in before—was, if anything, emptier. Even the dirty white blinds were gone. Steven looked out the window at the signs he'd seen the first time, at his car parked below, then walked the perimeter of the room, around the walls. He could see the scratches in the floor, the marks where the metal cabinets had rested. Bending down, he ran his fingers along the worn linoleum and found tiny slivers of copper, the barest reminder.

It had all happened, and this was where it had happened, but it seemed it would not happen here again. He had hoped they would be able to do it, that they could figure a way that Heather would be able to see—to see her self, even.

Standing, he returned to the hall, toward the stairs; at the last moment before descending, he stepped through the doorway of the first room. He hit the switch, and the lights came on, illuminating the cork walls, the colored pins scattered randomly, holding nothing. A feeling of helplessness passed over him, and a sense of disappointment. This was not just for Heather, but also for himself—now they would likely not do the thing that she had planned, the secret act that might allow her to see herself. He wondered if she would even tell him what this plan had been.

When Steven turned to leave the room, he saw that one red pin—next to the door, it had been behind him—pierced a narrow scrap of newspaper, an advertisement for a mattress company. He tore it loose, and turned it over; the other side was an article from a week ago, about a death at an electrical substation in Sellwood. A man named Victor Machado, on probation for child molestation, had been electrocuted. At the time of his death, the article said, he'd been under suspicion in the recent disappearance of a Portland juvenile, a boy named Leon Carmean.

Steven heard footsteps on the stairs. In a moment, the Asian man appeared in the doorway. He still wore his apron.

"Have you had any luck?" he said.

"This is all different," Steven said. "This has been changed all around."

"I'm sorry. I guess you were right." The man looked down at his feet; he wore rubber sandals, black socks. "I can't help you—I don't know anything about this."

"What?"

"I've never really been in these rooms. I do not know what business was done here."

Steven pinned the article back to the wall. "I understand that there are different rules," he said, "special ways of doing things that I'm not familiar with. Could you at least tell me where he went? When he left?"

"I can tell you what I know," the man said. "I have no

reason not to. Mr. Chesterton left two days ago, and said he would not return. He signed over the lease and sold the remaining goods to me. Then he stood on the sidewalk and watched as the men he hired removed everything from these rooms upstairs. Metal cabinets, cots, chairs and tables. Nothing special—they threw it all into a dumpster and took it away."

"I see," Steven said.

"It's not impossible that I might hear from him, but I don't expect to," the man said. "I wish I did know more—I have my own questions." He shrugged, and pointed at the stairs, turning away. "The door down there is open; I can't stay up here any longer—"

"I had hoped to make arrangements with Chesterton," Steven said, following the man. "That's all. Perhaps I could leave my name here, my number?"

"As you like," the man said.

28.

THE SKY WAS DARK, and Natalie's trailer looked damp and forgotten, rotting, settling into the ground. Kayla squinted as she stood under the cedar tree; she was checking for the truck's departing tire tracks—as if they would tell her something, if they were visible.

She stepped closer. Broken glass spread underfoot, yet the windows of the trailer seemed whole. She bent down, picked up a triangular shard. They were pieces of mirrors, strewn around with scraps of magazines, torn pages where she couldn't tell if she was looking at arms or legs, what parts of bodies the hair covered.

"Natalie?" she said, hardly shouting. The name didn't echo at all, as if it had never been spoken here, as if this were not a place she had ever lived.

The porch shifted beneath Kayla's weight; she heard the reaction inside, a sound like tearing paper, all the mice scrabbling on the floor and counters, trying to get to safety. The door was unlocked. When she hit the switch, she was half-surprised that the light came flickering on, illuminating the magazines strewn everywhere. White stuffing leaked from the couch and its cushions, out of holes where mice had already burrowed. Orange powder—Tang—had been spilled across the kitchen counter.

The black windows reflected back, and she saw herself—her arms out, her eyes wide, her hair sticking up in clumps—here, alone in Natalie's trailer. She breathed in, the air thick with mildew and dust, the sour smell of old magazines, mouse droppings.

The faceplates had been taken from the outlets, the exposed wires stripped of their insulation. The copper shone with a dull glow. She stepped through the hallway, into the bedroom, where there was nothing but a bare mattress and a wooden frame that had once held a mirror but now stood empty. Along the near wall, the metal door of the fuse box yawned half-open; on the floor, on the shelves were stacks of blown fuses—small round ones with their glass faces shattered, paper ones with holes torn in their sides. And thin copper wires dangled from the fuse box, hanging twisted along the wall as if they could be lifted and attached to something, bent around a wrist or finger.

Kayla heard a movement, a footstep, the rustle of paper.

"Hello?" she said. She held her breath and leaned against the wall, waiting.

"It's me," Chris said, from the other room.

He was sitting on the couch when she came through the doorway.

"Hey." He lifted his hand in a half-hearted wave. "No one's here. Nothing."

"I didn't know if you were coming," she said. "If you would come. I didn't see you at school."

"First day," he said. "Everything's mixed up."

Kayla stepped closer. She sat on the floor, on top of the magazines. She realized that all their covers had been torn off.

"Were you avoiding me," she said, "at school?"

"I was avoiding everyone," Chris said. "All anyone wants to talk about is Leon, and everyone's afraid to mention him, at the same time. They want to have a whole assembly, you know. Missing children and strangers, drugs—"

"Pathetic," Kayla said. "Everything's all torn up."

She put her left hand on the rubber toe of Chris's shoe, and turned the magazines' pages with her right. Men with mustaches were in all the advertisements; selling cigarettes, deodorants, CB radios. The people inside—Abbie Hoffman, Elton John, Ursula Andress—she had never heard of, and the middle of every magazine, where the centerfolds and the pictures had been, were all ripped out, missing.

"The only person who knows what happened to Leon," Chris said, "was that guy Victor."

"People say that," Kayla said. "I mean, that's depending

if Leon had anything to do with Victor, which I doubt."

"You don't think so?"

"It doesn't really matter," she said. "They'll never—we'll never find Leon."

"How do you know?"

"I just know."

Kayla stood up and sat on the couch, next to Chris. Their skateboards rested, wheels up, on the floor. On hers, the word BEWILDERED, where Leon had written it, was barely visible, almost entirely scratched away by rail slides and other tricks.

"We have to stay together," she said.

"I don't want to do that anymore," he said. "No more wires—"

"No," she said. "We didn't get enough, we didn't follow. Or even if we did, it'll take a while before we know, and especially then we wouldn't be able to tell. We wouldn't care."

"Let's just go," he said, standing, picking up his board. "There's nothing here."

The magazines slipped under their feet; they walked close together, their shoulders bumping, their arms brushing each other.

"I want to check this last room," Kayla said. "One second."

They stood in the doorway, waiting for the fluorescent light to flicker itself whole.

"What is it?" Chris said.

"Hardly anything left," Kayla said.

Twelve Styrofoam heads, three against each of the four walls, rested on the floor and stared at each other across the room. Some had faces painted on with fingernail polish and makeup, others were dented and missing noses, ears. Empty hooks marked the walls, and empty shoeboxes littered the floor, and—behind each bald, white head—four thumbtacks in the wall marked the corners of a long rectangle, where the centerfolds had hung. The heads had once held the wigs, all of Natalie's hair, and the hooks had held her clothing, the boxes her shoes. She had taken it all with her, wherever she had gone.

Kayla switched off the light, and followed Chris outside, across the yard and under the cedar tree, onto the gravel road. The moon was full, their pale shadows sliding along beside them as they walked.

"Maybe I didn't understand it right," Kayla said.

"It doesn't matter," Chris said. "It's over."

"It's not over," Kayla said. "No matter what, that's not true. Where we are now is slower, but still different, after everything that's happened. No one else is like we are."

They walked in silence, the ground turning from gravel to blacktop beneath their feet. Without speaking, they set down their boards and pushed off, sliding through the darkness. Chris followed Kayla, then Kayla followed Chris; their eight wheels echoed hollowly in the night air as they swept past dark houses, under the black shadows of trees.